Reign of the Vampire King

VAMPIRE KINGS
BOOK FIVE

RHIANNON FUTCH

For my Family,
Yes I am still doing the writing thing.
No, you should not read this one either.

Contents

One

Valdís

Breakfast has become my favorite time of day, except for one tiny little detail. Vincent. King Vincent the insufferable asshole. I try and try to not set him off but apparently he hates everything about me. So far this morning he hasn't shown up and I am beginning to have hopes that he will skip it today.

"How is the transfer of power going? Are Quorin and the others ready for the responsibility?"

Knox finishes his mouthful of food, "They are. I think they have made some great plans for the future of Atlantis and I am eager to let them have at it. We've been poorly managing this place for way too long. It will be good to have new leadership."

Vincent arrives at the table and pulls out a chair to sit, saying, "Yes, it will be good to be absolved of a responsibility we never should have been given to begin with."

Malic's eyes narrow, "Vincent, did you come to the table to start shit?"

Vincent's eyes seem to flash a different color, it happens so fast, I can't be sure it happened. "No Malic, I did not. It's no secret we shouldn't have been ruling all this time. Why is it any different for me to say it than Knox? Why aren't you mad at him?"

Malic sighs, "He didn't make it sound like our Goddess was an errant child in a position of power. Let's just finish our breakfast?"

We all tuck in to avoid the discomfort of a king behaving poorly and getting called on it in front of everyone. After a bit Chance asks, "Have you been able to find out anything more about what the Outsiders are planning?"

Shrugging, I reply, "I keep trying but it just seems like I am blocked from seeing them or something. I can't find and see pretty much anyone else. They are just darkness every time I cast the spell."

Malic nods, "That isn't surprising. He knows you are a witch. He wouldn't want you spying on all their plans. I would block you if I was him. I would also be preparing for war and I think we need to face the idea that we are likely to face a war here on our shores."

Vincent looks at me, "Will you and your witches be able to find some way to be useful at that point or will we be doing all the fighting again?"

Before I even think about it the words come tumbling from my lips, "The fuck is your problem, Vincent?"

He leans forward, "You. You are the reason for all of this. Had you not come running to the castle for saving, begging mercy from the only one of us likely to grant it, we wouldn't be in this mess to begin with."

Gage growls and Knox starts to speak but I hold up a hand, saying, "Knox, thank you but I would like to speak for myself here." He nods and I continue, "Vincent, I don't know why you seem to have such a vendetta for me. To be honest, I don't really care. I am going to give you fair warning. One more insult from you and you will find yourself dangling mid air until I decide to let you down."

Vincent's jaw drops, I watch his eyes as he looks at each of his fellow kings, searching in vain for support. Turning to my mother he says, "Are you really going to let your daughter speak to one of your kings like this?"

Dagma turns her eyes to her plate. Speaking softly she says, "She is a good woman with a kind heart, if she is rude to you, I know you have been atrocious to her. I should go. Excuse me."

She is out of her chair and gone before I can say anything. Unfortunately for Vincent, he now has the full attention of the two K's.

I'm frozen as I watch the two of them staring him down, until Gage and Knox stand in unison, Gage telling Vincent, "Come brother, we should become as scarce as the wolves. Before anything regrettable should happen."

Vincent stands with a snarl, "Fine, the food tastes bad anyway with such poor company as this."

The two K's look at Malic, "He is treading a thin line.

Dagma's control doesn't extend far where that one is concerned," Kalina says, gesturing at me.

With a weak chuckle I say, "I was more afraid of what you two were planning to do to him, once she left. You aren't planning anything retaliatory, are you?"

The innocent looks on their faces are just terrifying,

Malic tugs his collar, "Ladies, I would sincerely appreciate it if you could hold off on any possible actions that would cause us," he jerks a thumb to indicate himself, Chance, and me, "further issues. I am asking that you please give us time to take care of the problem before you do."

Kalina looks to Katerine. They don't speak aloud but I would swear they are talking to each other. Long moments later they look to Malic and Katerine says, "Agreed. We will give you time to course correct him. There is an end to our patience, he is making Dagma uncomfortable with her power and bullying our granddaughter. We are not taking this lightly."

"Understood and appreciated ladies. You are as generous as you are lovely, we are lucky to be graced with your benevolent presence."

They snort at his flattery but the struggle to keep from smiling is one they are losing. Kalina tries to look stern and fails, saying, "You are entirely too charming for your own good Malic. It is a good thing the castle parties stopped before I was old enough to attend. I would have given you such trouble. Come Katerine, let's go check on our Dagma."

Malic waits until they are out of hearing range, putting

his head in his hands he says, "Holy shit. I wasn't sure that would work. I don't know which one scared me more. The look in Dagma's eyes when Vincent was rude to you or the look on those two sweet old ladies' faces after Dagma left."

I shrug, "I'm not sure there is a safer option there. What is his problem anyway?"

Chance answers, "We don't know and he isn't talking. It could be anything, Maybe he is having trouble adjusting to being back. Maybe the scent of you is causing a war inside of him that we don't understand any more than he does."

Eirene

This palace life is the best. I never want to live anywhere but a palace ever again. Finishing my makeup for the day, I wander out into my bedroom. I can't seem to shake the thought that I need to finish off Atlantis, now. Not having been able to keep Valdís, our key, is bothering me greatly too.

I knew those damned kings would not give her up so easily. I'm sure that foolish cardinal paid for bringing her there.

I need to fix this. I need more information but my God can surely provide that. This is what he wants anyway. For me to finish what my family started so long ago. My parents weren't even the ones that took on the mission. It was my great, great grandparents. I feel certain it would have been many more generations between us had that cursed land not extended our lives unnaturally.

But that doesn't matter. None of it will matter if I don't get Valdís and destroy Atlantis. Calling my God is as easy as calling one of my guards from the other side of the door. He answers immediately, even before his form has finished appearing in my room, "How can I help you, darling one?"

Pacing as I talk I tell him, "I know that I need to finish the mission my family started so long ago, but I am at a loss. I don't know how to manage it. The kings are monsters in their own way, filthy blood drinkers. The whole place needs to sink into the ocean in fire and earthquakes the way that the history books said it happened. It's the ho—" I stop in my tracks, remembering that Eumeleia is still on the island. "What if I sent Eumeleia to the castle? She could infiltrate the palace and seduce the kings, distract them. We could send her to the castle under the guise of trying to find me. Valdís would have to take pity on her. And she is probably searching for me anyway."

He shakes his head no, "She isn't. She is sure you are hiding on that ridiculously big island somewhere and will come back when you feel it is safe. She took advantage of your absence and that of Ingemar to marry Pelos."

"She married him?" I shriek in a fury. "How could she! That fool! I had such great plans for her!" I start pacing again, mumbling about the many ways I want Pelos to die.

"You know, this works. She has always had a thing for that boy. If I send people to collect him, and bring him here, she will do whatever I tell her to in order to keep him safe. Yes! That will bring her to heel nicely."

He nods, "What else is troubling you?"

"The Organization. The cardinals have grown too used to being the power in the land and they are fighting me at every turn. I feel that it makes me appear weak if I have to call you in every time I deal with them. I, I need to do something to them that they won't forget for a very long time."

"I agree. You are going to need some more specialized types than the guards you are currently employing."

I stop and look at him, "Specialized? How? More training or something?"

He chuckles, "Or something indeed. It's time you learned about the monsters."

Two

Knox

I am happily doing paperwork when the three of them come in. Looking at their faces, I know this has to be about Vincent. His behavior this morning was so far out of character that there is no hope it could be ignored, though I would truly like to do just that. Standing, I ask, "Care for a drink to ease the troubles you brought in with you?"

Gage declines but Malic and Chance both nod their acceptance. It takes entirely too little time to pour three drinks and hand out the two that aren't mine. Seating myself behind my desk again I say, "I'm guessing you are here to talk about Vincent?"

Chance snickers as Malic glares at me, "Why else would we all gather up in here? Leaving her unprotected while he is wandering the castle? Leaving him unprotected while the two K's are wandering the castle? Do you know they didn't go back to the Witches Keep this morning? Those two are still wandering the halls here. Probably setting traps for the unwary."

He downs his drink and walks over to the bar to refill it. I raise a brow at Chance and he shrugs. I look over at Gage and he shakes his head no, saying, "The two K's appear to simply be haunting the palace. Just wandering the halls and watching. Vincent seems annoyed to be continually seeing them."

Malic seats himself across from me and I tell him, "I don't know what we can do about this. I know his behavior is nothing like the Vincent we know but what if he just changed? Maybe this shitty version of him is who he is now. Or maybe he just needs more time to get his shit together than we did. You know he has been avoiding coming home as much as he possibly could. I can't count the number of times that he called me to serve in his stead. I know I wasn't the only one he called."

"You weren't," Malic says, "but that isn't an indicator of this kind of personality change. It's like he's been on drugs this whole time, and that would be believable if they did anything at all for us. That would make sense. Paranoia will change the whole person in ways that seem unreal to the ones that knew them best."

Chance clears his throat, "I just don't see someone as straight-laced as he was ever being willing to start doing drugs."

"Stranger things have happened," I say with a wry smile. "But in this case, I think you all are correct, he isn't likely to have been on drugs this entire time. I think we just need to talk to him. Ask him some questions about things, before we make any assumptions that are going to really piss him off."

Gage nods his agreement, "He is right. If Vincent knew we were in here meeting about him, he would be very displeased. He will handle it much better if we speak directly to him. Probably."

Malic sighs, "You're right. Now the question is, who does honors?"

Chance and Gage are suddenly finding my walls and floor incredibly fascinating and I know with complete certainty that I have taken the bait for a trap. Dammit. "Fine. I'll do your damn dirty work. Asshole. Tormenting me with all this shit when you could have just gotten to the damn point twenty minutes ago, before you were drinking all my good booze."

Malic grins as he stands, "Excellent. I look forward to hearing what you find out." And with that he leaves, much faster than he entered.

✳ ✳ ✳

Valdís

· · ·

My guards are kind when I tell them I would prefer to ride in the backseat alone today and they don't argue. One of them opens the door to the backseat and holds it while I get seated. They always drive much slower than my kings do, being human with human reflexes. And maybe a little scared of what the kings would be like if I died and it was something they could have prevented.

The walls of the tunnel are smooth and not at all distracting as the vehicle moves slowly toward the palace.

Perhaps I should have sat up front and talked to the guards like I usually do. Then I wouldn't be seeing the women's faces. Three women we couldn't save today. One was dead when we arrived. Her throat had been cut after she was beaten severely and I can't bear thinking about what else may have happened. The other two, my heart broke for them. Still is breaking for them.

My mind keeps playing the looks on their faces as we told them we were there to help them. The horror. The fear as they looked to see if anyone else had seen us with them. The hatred as they condemned us, and themselves. The one, she knew. She knew exactly what she was.

She said she felt it when the power awoke within her, and knew it was evil. Evil! The power we are gifted isn't evil, we aren't evil. She's been working with the organization, helping them find other women like herself. She was going to give them a full report about seeing us. I tried everything to convince her that the power isn't evil. I even said our goddess's name out loud to her. I watched her stagger and then recover, shouting that I am evil incarnate and my tricks would not sway her faithful soul. She swore she would see me in one of the cages they use for the witches they catch.

I froze her heart in her chest. She clutched her chest for long seconds before she fell dead to the floor. Kneeling beside her I closed her eyes and steeled myself to face the women that were with me. They were kind, but it just made me feel worse. I set her home ablaze before we closed the portal.

The car slows and I realize we have arrived at the palace. Maybe I can make it to my room and shower the day away before my kings see me. I don't want them to worry and they would if they realized that I still go on some of the missions. I can't put all the responsibility for these women's lives on the other witches I work with, can't let them be the only ones feeling this hurt. Making these hard choices.

My guard opens the door and helps me out of the vehicle. The two of them walk with me to the door of the palace but excuse themselves from there, saying that they need to check in with Narich. I nod and wish them well as I enter the palace. The halls seem so long today. All I want is a shower to cry in before I see my kings. As soon as I smell Vincent I know my shower is going to be delayed.

He steps out of a doorway in front of me like he has been waiting for me to come through here just so he could stop me. "Where have you been all day?"

I am irrationally angry that I can't shout at him exactly what I was doing. I settle for saying, "I have been out watching people die. Now, as the day has been really long and awful in ways I dislike thinking about, I would really appreciate it if you could save this for another time."

"You were watching them die? What the hell is wrong with you? Why wouldn't you do anything to save them? What kind of evil are you? You are coming with me!"

I am stunned at him calling me evil and I watch in what seems like slow motion as he reaches out and grabs my arm. He is dragging me down the hall before I come to my senses and use the magic in me to freeze his legs in place from the hips down and set his hand on fire.

He lets go of my arm and I fall, hitting the floor hard. It brings tears to my eyes and I am even more angry that this bastard gets to see me cry now. He is cursing me, a steady stream of epithets listing my flaws and the amount of evil that must be lurking within me to have done what I did today, interspersed with demands to be released and threats of the dungeon. As if that could hold me.

I feel shaky as I get to my feet. I can't think with all the noise. Looking at him I cast the spell that silences him and the immediate silence is bliss as I try to get myself together. I think maybe I forgot to eat anything today after... the hot tears just flow faster down my cheeks. "You ever touch me again and I won't just set your hand on fire!" Yelling at him feels kind of good, "How dare you put your hands on me, be so fucking rude to me, when I tell you I have just had a really bad day! What the hell is wrong with you anyway? Have you always been this much of an entitled asshole?"

Malic is in front of me then, wrapping his big arms

around me, "What did he do to you? Are you ok? Why are you crying?"

"I'm crying because I had a bad day and this asshole made it worse. When he tried to drag me down the hall I set his hand on fire and then I fell and it hurt." Goddess I sound absolutely pathetic, "I- I'm fine though. I just need to go have a shower. That's all."

He rubs my back, "How many?"

I know he means how many witches couldn't be saved, "Three."

"Epaphras, come here."

Great, now he can see me crying too. Malic continues rubbing my back while he tells Epaphras, "I want you to walk with her to her room, if you see one of my brothers on the way call him over to be with her. It is likely they are looking for her now anyway. If you don't then track one down after you leave her at her room." He pulls back, his hands going to my shoulders, "My Queen, I need you to set Vincent free and let him speak again before you go with Epaphras."

I nod and wave a hand at him, releasing it all, but letting the ice turn to water instead of fading away.

Vincent immediately says, "It's about time you had that—"

Malic spins to face him, "Watch your tongue brother, before I decide to rip it out. You've done more than enough damage for today and you can be silent or we can test the strength of these walls with your head."

Vincent growls, "Fine. Get her out of my sight then."

Malic turns back to me, kisses my forehead and gives me a gentle push toward Epaphras. "Go my queen, I will see you soon." Epaphras puts an arm around my shoulder and guides me away, telling me it will all be okay.

I want so much to believe him, but how can it all be okay when even one of the kings thinks I'm evil? How long before they all think I'm evil?

Three

Malic

She looks so broken, of all the days for Vincent to act like this. I watch till she and Epaphras are out of sight before I turn my attention on Vincent, "What the fuck is wrong with you?"

Vincent stops trying to squeeze the water out of his pants to shout, "Nothing! She told me she had spent the day watching people die and I was bringing her to see all of you when she assaulted me. Obviously we can't have a murderous little bitch wandering the castle. What if she decided to murder one of our people? Maybe she is killing Epaphras right now!"

Rubbing my forehead with sigh, I try to breathe through the frustration. "Vincent, I don't know what is going on inside your head, but this isn't ok. You know she isn't some random woman walking around murdering people, like we do, I might add. More importantly, she is our queen. I know you know that. I know you remember things now that you have heard Hekate's name from her lips. Talk to me. What is happening? Why are you acting like this?"

His shoulders drop and he spreads his hands out in a gesture of not knowing, "I don't know. I'm hungry all the time and nothing seems to fill me. It's like a gnawing ache inside. My body hurts with the hunger no matter how much blood or food I take in. When I smell her it's like I can't control myself. Her scent sends a rage through me and I want to kill her as much as I want to fuck her. I, I don't intend to be so angry with her."

He looks away and I can see he is shamed by his own actions. "I want to help you. If there is something we can do that will help you through this, we are here for you. Is there a way we can help you?"

Vincent shrugs, "I don't know. Patience?"

I nod, "Of course. I can't promise that if you are violent with our queen. Or any of the witches. Let's just try to keep our violence contained. And for fuck's sake, please don't say rude things to Valdís in front of Dagma or the two K's."

He raises a brow at me, "Really? They worry you?"

I nearly jump out of my skin when the two K's speak from behind me, "We do, and with good reason."

As it is I spin around and step back, "Why the hell are you scaring me? Maybe a heart attack can't get me, but it sure doesn't fucking feel great. Fuck!"

They smile and reach out, each one patting one of my shoulders, "You're a dear boy. Don't you worry, we aren't here for you. We just wanted to help your friend under-stand what you were saying. I'd say he is having an epiphany right now."

I look over my shoulder at Vincent, he is pale. Fuck, I'm probably pale from the fucking scare they gave me. "Thank you for your help ladies, you are appreciated. Though I would greatly prefer that you don't scare anyone to death, a great many of the people here can die from a heart attack."

"Don't worry dear, we are very careful in regards to that. You boys have a nice day now."

We both watch the two of them walk off down the hall arm in arm, probably looking for their next victims. I realize that I am pressed up against Vincent still, I didn't even pay any attention to it when they appeared behind me. But now the back of my pants are damp from the contact. Stepping away from him I turn around and tell him, "Come on. Let's go get ready for dinner. Both of us need new pants. While we are at dinner you can work at being nice to Valdís and we will work on finding ways to remind you that are kind instead of curt. Maybe we should get you some more blood on the way."

Vincent shakes his head no as we start toward our rooms, "Don't you think I tried drinking extra? It isn't working."

"Were you starving yourself while you were gone?"

He scoffs, "Of course not! I ate rather well actually. There were always people lurking around the monastery."

I look at him, "Monastery?"

He nods, "Yes, don't worry, they had no idea who I was or what I was."

"Was it one of his? Is it possible that you were living in one of his houses of worship?"

He looks really uncomfortable now as he says, "I don't really know. I would swear I asked when I arrived, but I can't remember the answer. And I can't remember what the answer is from any other time I asked either."

I don't like this. I don't want to cause Vincent to feel any further shame or sadness or fear about this so I change the subject, but I have a feeling that we are going to need to investigate this further.

* * *

Eirene

Shoving my crown back where it is supposed to sit I ask Nicholas to repeat what he just told me.

Nicholas says, "Cardinal Abel and the rest of the cardinals have sent their regrets but they cannot attend the meeting you scheduled with them."

The adrenaline rushing through my body has my pulse pounding loud in my ears, I can barely hear Nicholas as he asks if I am all right, I wave him away, "Yes, yes, I am fine. I need to focus on destroying Atlantis, not fooling with these idiot Cardinals. I don't have time for this," I say as I slam my hand down on the table. Taking a calming breath, "Nicholas, I want you to contact every single one of those Cardinals and let them know that they will be at the meeting and they will be on time or I will have them collected and brought here to visit my dungeons until I decide to let them roam freely again."

He asks, "Are you sure? They have a formidable army at their disposal."

"I appreciate your concern Nicholas, but I found out this morning that I have a much larger and considerably more terrifying army at my disposal. One that has been instructed by our God himself not to follow any order that does not come directly from me."

His eyes go round and he nods, exiting to go make the calls. Edgar chuckles, "You won't make those Cardinals love you like this."

I turn and smile at him, "I don't want their love. They are foolish and fickle creatures. I would settle for their obedience. I'll take their fear. But they will learn who is in charge now or I will let them rot in the dungeons until I have both."

He asks, "Where did you find this army? Will I need to have the accountants get another payroll started?"

Shaking my head no I tell him, "This army isn't very interested in money. We should probably get a lot more meat into the kitchens though. Or maybe I'll start out feeding them Cardinals."

Twenty minutes later I am standing before a dais watching the Cardinals take their seats on the benches positioned in rows before me. I look toward the back of the room, where the shadows are deep. A single, small flash of light is all that I see, but that is enough. It reassures me that they are there. My attention is drawn back to the Cardinals as they whine and complain about the benches. Nicholas waves at me from behind them and gives me the signal to begin.

"Gentlemen, Cardinals, if you prefer your titles. I am so pleased you could make it here today, I know you all were very busy. Do not despair of falling behind in your ever so important work, forgive me, I am still learning the ways of my land. What is it you do for our people?"

Cardinal Morrow stands, "This is outrageous! How can you think that we would do as you say and you don't even know the ways of our lands? You are presumptuous and ill-mannered. What do we do indeed!"

I smile at him, "Well, I understand how you might feel that way. The thing is, I have been studying the ways of our lands—"

Cardinal Crane shouts, "Then you know the monarchy was never actually meant to rule!"

"I know if you dare to interrupt me again I will have your head removed from your body and I will make everyone here watch. Now, as I was saying before I was so rudely interrupted, in all my studying, I have yet to find exactly what it is that you do. And that bothered me. I read all about what I as the ruling power in this land needs to manage, which actually includes you. Yet, your duties were not clearly stated anywhere. That—"

"Is none of your concern," Cardinal Basillis snarls at me, "I am done with this farce. This pretense of your power. You have none. You will never have any power in this land, and your attempts to force us to buy into it are laughable."

For just a second, as he started to walk away, I almost believed him. The smallest of lights caught my attention from the shadows in the back of the room and I remembered why I called them here. With the brightest smile I can paste on my face I say, "Gentlemen, do wait one moment, I would hate for you to miss out on the surprise." They turn to look at me, annoyance writ plain across their faces as I lift my arms slowly above my head and quickly bring them down to my sides. My monsters come marching out of the dark. Mostly, they look like men. Until you catch just the right angle, where the illusion is thin and you can see the monster underneath. The teeth, fur or sometimes scales. A few have both. The claws attached to fingers still capable of firing a gun. The Cardinals are stunned, watching as my monsters surround them. "Gentlemen, or Cardinals if you prefer that still, my people are here to invite you for a stay in the palace. Thanks to the good Cardinal Abel, I am fully aware that you have not been really consistent in fulfilling your duties to our God. You are all quite unsanctified as you haven't been performing your rituals. We, our God and I, have decided you need some time to get back to your spirituality. To really reconnect with our God. Time for prayer and ritual and really focusing on your religious duties to our God."

They all start shouting at that point and I chuckle at their display. When I have grown tired of it I look at one of my monsters and nod, he smiles and roars at the Cardinals.

The silence that follows is sheer bliss, though the smell coming from one of the Cardinals now is less than blissful. "Please do take the Cardinals to where they will stay for the next little while. And gentlemen, you should do exactly as you are told or you may not make it to the dungeon. Don't worry, whatever is left will be used in the compost."

The cardinals pale as a group, well, except the one that is bright red with his embarrassment. My monsters split into groups, one that leads them toward the exit and another that follows. Looking to Nicholas I say, "Could you make certain that the one gets fresh clothing and is able to cleanse himself? I won't put him through remaining soiled. That would be too cruel. Oh, and make sure they have all the supplies needed for their sanctifying rituals and worship in general." He nods and pulls out his phone. Edgar walks over and offers his hand as I step down from the dais.

Four

I ngemar

We are all moping in our corners, so to speak, when the monsters walk in. Kleitos looks around and sidles over a little closer. Judda starts panting, breathing like he has run a mile. The monsters sniff the air and smile. So many teeth. How can they have so many teeth in one mouth? My heart feels like it will beat out of my chest. I try to slow my breathing to keep calm.

It isn't working.

I do manage to stay seated and keep my muscles lax to appear as though everything is fine. Kleitos is doing the same, as are most of the lords. Except Judda. Judda's eyes are darting around the room like a rat in a cage and I have a real bad feeling about him. The monsters unlock the cage and open the door as they say, "Ingemar, Kleitos, you're coming with us." We start to stand but Judda leaps to his feet, shrieking, "No! I have to get out of here! You take me to see that bitch! I am a lord! She knows who I am and you," he steps forward and pokes one of them in the chest, "are nothing to me. Get out of my way! I'll go find her myself." I watch in horror as he tries to shove past them. They don't move and he loses his mind, hitting and kicking them. I turn away when one of them smiles. Too many teeth. The sounds, oh goddess, the sounds. His screams were cut off almost instantly. The bile rises in my throat when I realize what the sounds are, they are chewing sounds. They are eating Judda. I can only hope he died quickly. He probably died about the time the screams were cut off, yes. That is what I am going to believe. The the sounds have faded to nothing I force myself to look, there is so much blood. So much blood. They are just standing there watching me, waiting.

"You, erm, hm." I have to try a second time as my stomach is still pretty fucking jumpy. "Before the, uh, the disturbance, you said Kleitos and I were coming with you. Do you still wish us to do so?" They nod and I carefully stand, turning to give Kleitos a hand up. We are both more than a little shaky but shove it down to walk as normally as possible. We exit the cage, careful not to seem aggressive or like we might try to run away. The one monster closes the door to the cage while the other leads the way, motioning for us to follow him.

Eirene

. . .

I've started calling this room my map room. The focus of the room is a large world map, a very old one that has been restored and glass set over it. This map is so old that it still shows the location of Atlantis. Since I arrived we have set up a second table with the maps I brought with me. While they aren't world maps, they are maps of Atlantis that will help when I send my monsters there. And when I send my men there to collect that wretched Pelos. I can't believe Eumeleia went behind my back and married him. Ew. He was such a disgusting boy.

It's fine though. He will make a perfect tool for making Eumeleia do whatever I tell her to do. She had become less and less cooperative after Valdís was taken from Ingemar's home. I think they are likely living in Ingemar's home. Which, luckily, isn't far from mine should my guess be wrong.

Nicholas steps up beside me as I stare down at the street map of the town where Eumeleia is still. "You don't think she will cooperate without the removal of her husband?"

"No, I know she will not cooperate unless we give her a reason to do so. She is obviously going through a rebellious phase and I will need to keep her convinced. Having Pelos as hostage will do just that." I point at the area where Ingemar's home is, "They are likely staying in this home, but if they are not, then my home is just down the way here. I want a team sent there. They can collect Pelos, give my daughter a phone and teach her the basics of how to use it, and she can keep me updated as to what is going on in that castle of theirs."

He nods, "Very well. Do you want them all human or a mix?"

I pace a little as I think about that, "I think perhaps it should be a mix. That way my monsters will have an opportunity to get a feel for the place. Before they destroy it completely when they return for the last time."

"Very we--," he cuts off whatever he would have said when my monsters walk in with Ingemar and Kleitos in tow. Which is what I asked them to do, but their uniforms are dripping blood everywhere.

"What happened?"

The lead monster, Harry, answers, "One of the prisoners got mouthy and tried to break out. We fixed the problem."

"That's fine, but why are your uniforms so filthy?"

He shrugs, "We're messy eaters?"

I feel my eyes roll of their own accord and I tell him, "Go change your uniform. Send those to be cleaned. It's fine to be a messy eater, I'm sure that has an effect on morale for the ones that need a lesson. But you absolutely must change uniforms afterward. Messy is fine, sloppy is not."

"Yes ma'am. Will you be wanting replacements to keep these two in line while we are gone?"

I look at Ingemar and Kleitos, they both look a bit shaken still, "I think they will behave, knowing what you could and would do to them should you return to find that they didn't."

They smile at Ingemar and Kleitos before they turn and leave to change. Once they are out of the room I turn back to the map and wave the other two over. "Ingemar, our children are married. I need Eumeleia to do some things for me. We are going to collect Pelos and bring him here as leverage. Which house do you think the happy couple will be staying in?"

Ingemar is quiet long enough that I look at him and he seems to be thinking hard. He finally says, "I feel certain that they will stay in what was my home. Pelos will want to be close to where his mother was and will feel responsible for making sure his mother's legacy continues on."

That is a strange way to phrase that, "What do you mean, his mother's legacy?"

He steps a little closer, leaning in like he is telling a secret, "Well, I married into the family. My family was minor nobility at best. We were not landed nor wealthy. Her family had those things and a higher title. When her father passed away there was, conveniently, no other man left to inherit but me. Since her father was very certain that only a man could run his estates properly, he left me in charge, passing titles and everything else to my control with the stipulation that if I divorced his daughter it would all revert to her."

I laugh, "Is that why she had to die? Very poor form, dragging it out for all those years. Why not let her die already?"

"She was just damn tough. It wasn't for lack of trying on my part, I assure you."

"I see. Can you draw out the layout of your home?"

* * *

Pelos

I should be in bed with my Eumeleia. She has been asleep for an hour now. But I must get this letter to the kings just right. I need them to understand, for Eumeleia to be safe. It's nearly there, just a few more little tweaks and then I can write it out again without all the edits.

Just as I pull out another sheet of paper my office door bursts open, letting monsters and men stream through the opening. I leap to my feet and look for a weapon, but it's my father's office, there are no weapons in here. And they are upon me before I can do anything. The faces of the ones holding me are strange, a combination of man and beast. A regular man stands before my desk and he asks, "Are you Pelos?"

"No, I am just the butler. What are you doing in here? Sir Pelos will be very angry when he finds you in his home."

He raises a brow and nods, one of the monsters holding me slaps my face. I taste blood as the man before me says, "Pelos, I don't like being lied to, don't do it again. Now, where is your darling wife? Rest assured, she will remain unharmed. It is your life that is at risk, not hers."

Well they can have my life, "She is asleep in our bedroom." We walk up the stairs and to my bedroom door where I ask, "Could you please knock, give her some sort of notice that it isn't me walking in." It's then that I realize they didn't ask me how to find our bedroom.

The man nods and gives the door a couple sharp raps before turning the knob to open the door and walk in. My Eumeleia is sitting up in the bed, bleary eyed until she sees the monsters holding me. Scrambling out of the bed, she hurries toward us.

Five

Eumeleia

I know this is my mother's doing as soon as I see the men, the monsters, holding my Pelos. "What does my mother want?"

The man leading them in smiles, "Ah, good. She said you would know she had sent us. Then you will also know we aren't lying when we say that if you do not do exactly as you are told he will die."

"Yes, I understand. What am I to do?"

One of the monsters says, "Get on your knees, Princess."

The man with them says, "No, that is not part of the plan! This is the Queen's daughter, she is due some respect. Eumeleia, do you know what a phone is?"

"A what? No, I don't."

He mumbles something about backwater places as he walks over, pulling a small rectangle from his pocket.

Extending his hand he flips the rectangle open and explains, "This is a phone," and he goes over how to use it. I work hard at memorizing the instructions, making him go through them again and again till I have it. Then we practice using it. He sends me a message, calls me, and we go over it until I am confident I won't forget how to use it. Once that is settled he says, "Now, your job is to get into the castle with the kings. Befriend them. When the time comes you will cause a disturbance and keep them very distracted. Your mother doesn't care how you do it, only that it is done. You will be messaged daily to call us and report. The number to call is saved in your phone, can you find it?"

I quickly look through the phone and find where the number is saved, "Yes, I found it."

"Very good. When will you leave for the castle?"

Pelos breaks then, "Don't do it Eumeleia, just let me die."

My darling Pelos, he doesn't understand my mother at all. I walk over to him and put my hands on either side of his face, looking up into his eyes, "Love, all that would accomplish is your death. My mother would find another way to force me to do what she wants. This is the only way for me to ensure you live." I turn back to the man, "I have a demand."

He chuckles, "Ok Princess, tell me, what is your demand?"

"I must call daily anyway, as part of that I need to speak to Pelos everyday as well."

He nods, "I think that will be allowed. The final decision will rest with your mother."

"You can tell Mother that if Pelos dies, all of her plans will die with him. I am her daughter, and while I choose to be different, it isn't for a lack of ability to be as evil as she is. Without Pelos, I will make it my life's mission to see her every plan, every dream, all of it come crashing to an end so I can watch her misery."

His eyes widened at that, "Very well Princess, I will relay your demand to your mother. She won't be happy about it."

"I am well aware of how my mother will feel. You should ensure that she is well aware of how serious I am about this."

Knox

We are having a discussion with Vincent about what the hell is up with him when Epaphras knocks and enters, "Your Highnesses, we have a petitioner."

He looks wildly uncomfortable and Epaphras is mostly unflappable, "What is it? What is the weirdness with this one? The last time you were bothered it was Valdís."

He nods, "Yes. Indeed. Well, it is her stepsister."

Chance stands, "What? Why would she be here, of all places? Is her mother with her?"

Epaphras says, "I know, it is strange. Her mother is not

with her. She says that her mother took her husband, Pelos. Ingemar's son. My intel says they did recently marry. Her mother has not been seen since someone reported watching her boarding a boat some time ago. Do you want to see her or should I send her on her way?"

Vincent says, "When have we ever turned a petitioner away without at least hearing them out?"

Epaphras presses his lips together, "I can think of three from the last time you were here."

Vincent flushes a deep red, "We will see her regardless."

"As you wish sire. In the throne room?"

Vincent snarls, "Yes! Now go! You bother me with your questions and insinuations!"

"I apologize Epaphras, my brother is not well today, please forgive us all his behavior and know that we are working to adjust it."

He nods, "Thank you sire. She will be waiting for you all in the throne room."

Once the door shuts behind him I turn to Vincent, "What the hell are you doing being shitty to Epaphras?"

Vincent runs a hand over his face, "I don't know. I was already annoyed and it just boiled over. I'll apologize to him myself later. Let's go to the throne room."

As we walk I fill him in on the details about Eumeleia that he needs to know, like the fact that Conrí is not her father, can't be. He is skeptical that the Conrí he knew could have married an Outsider and no one noticed. We do our best to assure him that is the case, especially as we all saw her leaving the field in front of the castle, the Outsiders following her orders.

Vincent

My brothers are surely delusional. There is no way that we have had that many Outsiders living here all this time, pretending to be one of us. Hiding the mark every day? That's so much work. I can't see why anyone would choose to do it. We enter the throne room and a scent hits me, it's different. Almost hypnotic, nothing like Valdís's scent that stirs me and riles me all at the same time. It's sweet and soothing. My brothers are coughing next to me, "What is your problem? Why are you coughing like that? Get it together."

Knox clears his throat and pulls his shirt up over his nose, "Don't you smell it? That cloying, choking scent?"

My face scrunches, "What are you talking about? I smell a nice perfume, it's actually kind of soothing." I watch him meet eyes with Chance and I feel like I should be concerned. I'm sure it will all be fine as I inhale deeply of the scent in this room.

Epaphras has three thrones at the spot where generally only one sits. It is a curious thing to see after so long. Not twelve and not one. The woman comes to stand before us and tells us of how her mother has sent people to take her dear husband Pelos and refuses to give him back. She insists we must do something about this as it wouldn't have happened were it not for this silly war between the two lands, and we are directly responsible for her husband's life. I can't help but agree with a story so compelling as hers. Chance says, "There is a lie in there somewhere. What are you lying about? Is it that your mother took him? Did he go willingly to provide you with a reason to come here? Or is it that you know we are not in any way responsible for your mother's actions?"

I can't believe Chance said that to this poor, sweet lady! "Chance! Mind your manners! Eumeleia, of course you will stay with us until such time as we can find some way to bring your husband home safely. Epaphras, please show Eumeleia to a room. She will be staying with us for a time while we investigate the disappearance of her husband." Epaphras looks like he has swallowed something that is trying to escape the confines of his throat as he stares at me, wide eyed. "You heard me, find her a room." He gets himself together and I watch him as he escorts her from the room.

Malic

I am reading reports in my office when Epaphras comes bursting in, "Sire, forgive me, but I have important news."

"Come in, Epaphras, you are always welcome in here. What is the problem?"

"Valdís's stepsister, Eumeleia, is here. She came as petitioner and King Vincent has ordered that she stay until we find and fetch home her husband. But that isn't the part I need to tell you. Sire, she has a phone on her person."

Leaning forward I say, "What? I think I didn't hear you right. Did you say she has a phone?"

"I did. She brought a phone into the castle with her."

"I see. Does anyone else know?"

"Your brothers Knox and Chance were there with King Vincent when he walked over them and ordered that she stay, Gage is with Valdís today."

"Don't mention this to anyone. Are we still monitoring everything that comes in or goes out of here electronically?"

"We are, and everything is still being recorded."

"Good. Watch Eumeleia's and keep me informed as to what she is doing here. And let's keep that between us as well. The less that know, the better we can plan around their plans. Incidentally, has Vincent made any calls out?"

"No sire, should I inform you if he does?"

"Yes, I think maybe until his strange behavior is resolved, you should."

Valdís

My witches have been training hard, and it shows. I am so proud of the progress we have all made with our magic. My magic is fully under my control at this point and I am relieved. Now we spend a lot of time making sure that everyone can control their magic because even small magics out of control have consequences. I am watching a group link their magic when I see Chance and Malic come out of the keep and start walking toward me. Turning to my mom I excuse myself, "I'll be back. They look serious. You've got this, right?"

Dagma says, "Of course, go. We'll be fine."

Hugging her, just because I can, I whisper "Thank you." Releasing her, I turn and walk over to meet them before they get too close to the women linking their magic. Less distraction while they do that the first few times is always better. Besides, sometimes their magic is not compatible and the results of that are always forceful.

They hug me and I am surrounded by muscles and fantastic scents. I could stay here forever. Eventually though, they release me and Malic asks, "Do you have a little bit to go somewhere out of hearing range and talk?"

"I do, mind if it is just the far side of the courtyard? I want to stay close in case anything happens. Mixing magics can be explosive sometimes."

Chance laughs, "I'm not at all surprised. Why are you mixing magics?"

"Range and effect. When we combine our magics everything gets a boost. We are finding that we can't just combine everyone with no order. So we are experimenting with small groups linking and then linking the small groups into larger ones. We haven't quite gotten to the point of everyone being linked but we are working toward it. Working it that way seems to be working the best, so far. More importantly, I can see and smooth things over if things get a little frazzled with the groups linking. I seem to be able to link with all of them at will without ill affecting the stability of the group as a whole."

We have been walking as I spoke and now are in a small grouping of trees. I use my magic to keep our conversation private, creating a sound bubble around us. When I finish, Malic erupts, "It's about Vincent. He isn't usually like this. His behavior is far out of the range of normal for him and we are worried. And, you need to know that Eumeleia is at the castle; with Vincent's blessing."

My blood feels frozen in my veins. It must have shown on my face because Chance tugs me over to lean against him, his arms around me and hands clasped, resting on my belly. "Why is Eumie at the castle?"

Malic shoves a hand through his hair, "We aren't entirely sure." He tells me about the story she told them of Eirene taking Pelos from her and that part of her story is a lie. I look toward the women still practicing and I see Gage sitting outside the bubble, watching. He is in his wolf form today. He says he likes to check the courtyard with his other nose, and the other women will ignore him when he is in that form. Lifting my hand I create a space in the bubble for him to enter, closing it after he walks through. He shifts and I call in a pair of pants for him. He hates the idea of people staring at him after he changes and though naked-ness doesn't bother him, the piece of clothing helps him feel less seen.

"Well, I can honestly say that Eumie has always loved Pelos. Since the day she met him. Eirene would have no problem taking Pelos and holding him hostage if it would make Eumie do what she was told. She did it with her favorite things all the time. I don't know if Eumie even real-izes that she stopped having favorite things when she was still a child. She never was able to hide how much she like Pelos. If I had to guess, the part of her story that is a lie is that she believes you all to be responsible for it. She was sent here for a purpose. It is very likely that Pelos is the favorite toy being held over her head."

I feel Chance nod behind me, "I think you are probably right. The question is, why was she told to come here?"

Malic nods, "Exactly. What is Eirene planning? This is why we don't have time for Vincent to be acting so strange."

"Maybe we should get Dagma to scan him sometime soon? She is really good at seeing things in the body and figuring out what is going on." I look over at Gage with a smile, "Or seeing things that not many others can see."

Gage smiles and Chance says, "Indeed. I think having Dagma scan him is a good idea. Maybe she could scan him when you aren't around?"

Chuckling, I say, "That might be a good idea."

Malic nods, "Hopefully she can find out what is wrong with him."

Seven

Valdís

My mind has been half on Eumie all day. Why is she here? What is Eirene up to now? There is no way Eumie believes the kings are responsible for what her mother has done. I see Epaphras walking through the halls and I stop him, "Would you know where Eumeleia is?"

He frowns, "King Vincent gave her the run of the castle. She is currently in the pink sitting room. There are guards following her, please do pretend they are not following her. They are not there for her protection."

"I understand. Thank you." I head for the pink sitting room, I can't imagine why there is a pink sitting room. None of the kings are especially fond of the color. I've been in each of their rooms, none of them has so much as a pink throw pillow. Well, except Vincent. I haven't gone any closer to his room than passing it in the hall. Perhaps they thought they were creating a sitting room for their future queen. I walk in, oh sweet Lady, the whole room is shades of pink. So. Much. Pink. Eumeleia jumps when she realizes I am there, her movement takes my focus off the room as she asks, "What are you doing here?"

I tilt my head, "I live here?"

She scowls, "I mean, what are you doing here in this particular room?"

"Oh! Well, I heard you were here and I came to find you." I walk over and sit in the chair across from her, "Are you okay? You married Pelos? Congratulations on your marriage, I'm so sorry your mother took him away from you."

Eumeleia's face pales and even I can almost smell the stench of fear coming from her. She lifts her chin, "She took him because of you!"

My jaw drops, "What? Have you been drinking? That's ridiculous, I had nothing to do with your husband being taken by your mother."

She leans toward me, her face an odd expression of fear and rage, "He wouldn't have been kidnapped if you had just stayed there and helped our mother with whatever she needs from you. Now I have to suffer too!"

I jerk back as though she slapped me with those hateful words. Does she not know? What if she does? What if she really expected me to just die for her mother's plans? "You are either an ignorant fool or a selfish brat. We will work to get your husband back, but it will work so much better if you give us more information. If you could provide a bit of Pelos, hair or nails or favorite shirt or something, we can probably find out where he is fast and be able to bring him to you."

She leans back and looks away, "I have nothing of him."

I know she is lying. I saw her collecting bits of him before my father died. "That's a lie Eumeleia, and I won't pretend it isn't. I saw you collecting bits of him even before my father died. Why are you lying when this would help you get him back?"

Tears start pouring from her eyes as she stands, "You can't help and you wouldn't understand! Your just the useless child of a maid who couldn't keep her legs shut anyway!"

I laugh before I can stop myself, "Do you even know who your father is?" She flinches and I continue, You don't want my help, that is fine." I stand, looking down at her now, "If I catch you doing anything that will hurt my kings or this land, I will end you. However, if you change your mind about the help and choose to provide a small piece of him, that you will get back, I will do my best to find him and bring him back safely to you. Life and our parents ensured we wouldn't be friends, but I don't hate you Eumie. I would see you happy if it is within my power."

She sniffs, dashing away the tracks of her tears though more are falling. "The best way for you to fix this is to go do whatever mother is asking of you and leave me out of it."

She marches out of the room, leaving me standing there like the fool I am.

* * *

Eirene

The castle is buzzing with the news that my people have brought a prisoner from Atlantis. Ingemar and Kleitos are here with me as I wait to greet Pelos in my throne room. I have a special room prepared for him, away from the rest of the rabble I have inhabiting my dungeon. After all, it is possible that Eumeleia will get to come here and keep her husband and I want to have him hale and healthy for her. She will need to have an insemination done at some point if she plans to have children and she will have to have at least one. The royal line must be carried on and it doesn't matter whether the child is male or female as long as it is of our line.

Pelos is brought in by two of my monsters and judging by the look of him, he was well behaved for the entire trip here. "Welcome Pelos, I trust the journey was not terribly taxing for you?"

He frowns, "The trip was fine, being kidnapped and used as a tool to blackmail my wife is the terrible part. How could you do that to your own daughter?"

"Ingemar, do take your son down to the room I have prepared for him and perhaps explain to him just how things are here. I would hate for him to have an... accident."

Ingemar stammers, "Yes, I mean, yes your highness. Right away."

He walks out, leading the way. My two monsters get Pelos turned and start him walking when he plants his feet to say, "I hope you lose. I hope everything you touch turns to dust in your hands and that dust flies in your eyes to blind you. I hope that whatever happens to me, your daughter lives a long, happy life without your evil."

I laugh as one of my monsters punches him in the gut. He is struggling to breathe as they take him away. Nicholas comes in to report, "My man tells me your men were lewd with your daughter, you may want to speak with them about that. And he says that your daughter had one demand. She says that since she is to call and check in daily, she needs to speak to Pelos daily as well."

I laugh some more, "Very well, she can speak to her Pelos every day, after she speaks with me. I will have someone take the phone down there to him. I am glad to see she is at least trying to be clever and proactive. It does me proud. Perhaps she will manage to be a worthy successor." I am still laughing as I pull out my phone and send her a message instructing her to call.

Pelos

They have to drag me part of the way to the cell after knocking the air out of me. My father simply walks along ahead of me like nothing happened. I don't know why I am surprised. He never cared one way or another. And now here he is, in the land of the Outsiders, Eirene's stooge.

They are none too gentle when they toss me into the cage she had set up for me. It looks like a new set up. I guess I should be honored that she had something new set up for me, but it isn't really feeling like an honor while I am on my hands and knees gasping for air.

I hear the door clang as they close it. I have hopes that everyone has left but no. When I finally struggle to my feet, father is still there, waiting. As I stand there trying to get my breathing fully under control again he says, "It is good to see you son."

I use my first full breath to say, "I wish I could say the same, instead I really just wish you would fuck all the way off."

He sighs, like I'm some big fucking burden to him, "Son, I'm making the best of a situation I have no control over. Surely you understand the position I am in."

"The position you are in? Which one would that be? The position where you tried to lead a rebellion and were outsmarted by the woman you looked down on? That one? Or is it the position where you ended up in the land of the Outsiders because you, even after finding out you were not in the position of power you thought you were in, still went to try to battle the kings thinking you would have some sort of coup? Or, or, maybe it's the position that originally led you here. The one you put yourself in by murdering my mother." His jaw goes slack and his eyes round, "Oh yes father, I know. I know what you did. That you are so despicable you would murder the woman that loved you beyond all reason simply so that no one could take your supposed power from you. And now, now you have no power because you are ridiculously greedy and the power you were granted by marriage to my mother wasn't enough for you, even after her death. What I want to know is, did you ever care for her at all? Or was it always about the power?"

He shakes himself and takes a breath, "No. I was never in love with her. I married her solely for the wealth and title she could provide. She loved the person I pretended to be and as that faded, she loved that I had given her you."

"Oh father, it really is a shame that you are so convinced of your own grandeur that you honestly never figured it out, did you?"

"Figured out what, Pelos?"

"That I am not your son. That you have never had nor will you ever have a child of your line. Mom told me on her deathbed who my father is. He has been working for you all these years and has no idea that I know. And now, you are going to know. I hope it eats you up inside that Hulthen is my father."

He clutches his chest and throws a hand out to brace against the wall. If he dies of an attack here in front of me because of what I just told him, I'll consider this a good day. He is red in the face and gasping, "Hulthen? No! It can't be! She was such a good girl and Hulthen was my best servant!"

I smile, "He certainly was, he was so good that he even kept your wife happy when you could not. She said he pleasured her in ways you never did."

My mother never said any such thing but maybe it will push him over the edge and he'll die here on the floor while I watch. Sadly, he regains control and all the red fades from his face. Just another way he has disappointed me today.

Crossing my arms over my chest, I simply wait as he stands there gathering his thoughts. Finally he says, "Well, as far as I am concerned you are still my son as I raised you and I am going to choose to believe she lied to you." I laugh and he scowls at me, "If you speak of this to myself or anyone else again, I will have you beaten within an inch of your life."

I tilt my head to one side, "And you think Eirene will allow that? Are you not aware of why I am here? Ingemar, you are still overestimating your power and ability to control others. Get out of here, you are tiresome and I would rather stare at the wall than your murderous countenance."

Eight

Valdís

I love these gardens. I found a spot that has a small gazebo, just big enough to be a large alcove if it were indoors. The gazebo is covered over with jasmine and smells divine. The scent of the flowers seems to have soaked into the wood as it is scented whether or not the vines are in bloom. Even the opening is mostly draped with vines. It is always cool and dark, it just has a welcoming feeling that soothes my soul when I am feeling rough around the edges or just plain heartsick from seeing yet another dead witch. Or being the one to kill another witch. Her death still haunts me, even though I know it was the right thing to do. Better still, if I am in here, Vincent usually won't notice me. The scent of jasmine flowers seems to cover mine enough that he can ignore it and I am grateful for the break it gives me, if I can get out here without him seeing me.

I see Knox walking up the path and I debate on whether

I want to let him know I am here. The debate is moot once he lifts his nose, inhaling deeply and then looks directly at my little hiding space. He stops outside of it, still on the path, "Can I come in or would you rather be alone?"

I love how considerate he is, now. "You can come in."

I am always a little amazed at how these big men are able to move so gently through the world. He seems to almost float over the thyme and clover ground cover. I scoot over on the bench so he can sit next to me and he asks, "So, why are you hiding out here?"

"I just needed to be in my spot. This week has been really hard, with the deaths and the nonsense. Sometimes I need this spot, this dark and welcoming space. I've always felt safer in dark spaces, because the monsters in my life have been really good at hiding themselves in the brightest of lights."

He nods and puts an arm around me, "I understand. Well, as much as I can. I can see it has been hard on you and I am sorry for that."

"I appreciate that. But let's talk about something else. Something happier. How is the Witches Council doing?"

I can almost feel the happiness coming from him as he says, "They are going to do amazing things for our land. Quorin has a brilliant mind and she is spearheading some things that will do wonders for the lives of everyone here. And, they are talking about revealing ourselves to the world. We'll need to get Hekate to ok that, as she is the one that hid us from everyone. But, as the God of the Outsiders is helping them get here to attack and harass us, I think hiding isn't really an option anymore. Even Vincent supports their ideas."

"Aw, that is wonderful. I love seeing Quorin finally get to thrive and not live in fear anymore. She is glowing these days, at least she is the little bit that I see her. She is usually practicing her craft in the evening before she and Lommán retire for the night."

He gives me a little squeeze, "She has said many times that she wishes you would join the council."

"I know. I just think I shouldn't. I am too closely tied to you kings and I don't want anyone thinking that I am pushing your agenda, or using that as an excuse to shout down something I want to get done. What if my being part of the council makes our people believe that the Witches Council is just a front? I feel like it will be better if I stay as far out of the running of the country as you all are working on being."

"You are right, of course. Our people would not always be able to see you as separate from us which would cause the council and you plenty of issues that you don't need. Not to mention, you have this whole thing with the God of the Outsiders wanting to use you for a power source."

"Exactly that. That is plenty to deal with all on it's own."

He scoops me up and deposits me in his lap, holding me close. I love it. I haven't yet gotten to a point where I can just ask for it, but when they decide it is time, I am always happy for the closeness. I tuck myself into him, squirming around to lean my head on his shoulder and just breathe him in. He murmurs, "Um, maybe squirm less on my lap? I want to be supportive and not try to distract you with sex but you're making it very hard."

Giggling, I squirm a little more, "Perhaps that is just the distraction I need? Get me out of my head and into my body."

"I am here to serve however you need, and I would love to taste you."

I have never been so happy to have worn a skirt in my life. Lifting my head, I look him in the eyes and whisper, "I'm not wearing anything under this skirt."

And just like the he lifts me into the air, holding me up until I get my feet under me. Next thing I know he has one of my feet on the bench and he is under my skirt, his lips and tongue working a magic of their own. My standing leg starts to tremble and he rucks my skirt up farther to put a hand on either side of my waist and lifts me up to set me down very gently on the bench. As soon as I am supported by the bench one of his hands leaves my waist only to sink two fingers into my hot, wet, sheath. His tongue plays me till I am moaning will pleasure as his fingers glide slowly in and out. It's heaven and hell all rolled into one, "Oh Goddess, Knox, please!"

I hear the growl from his throat and his fingers finally give me the friction I need to sail right over the cliff's edge into oblivion. He pulls his fingers out of my core with an excruciating slowness, I could die from the waves of ecstasy the movement sends through me.

When they are gone I feel empty and I want that full

feeling back, I want to ride those waves. I look up at Knox from my position, leaned back on the wall of this small gazebo, to whisper, "Knox, I need you."

He unbuttons his pants with an agonizing slowness. I am mesmerized as he reveals himself. His pants open, he shoves them down far enough to be out of the way and fists his cock to line it up with my core. He tries to go slow but I wrap my legs around him, driving him to bury himself within me. He has me gasping at the sensations as he leans down to snatch me up into his arms, pounding his cock into me hard and fast.

He sinks his fangs into that sensitive spot where neck and shoulder meet causing a burst of pleasure that explodes into a climax rocketing through my body even as I feel him joining me in this sweet oblivion.

Eirene

Ingemar and Kleitos are in the dining room when I arrive. Taking my seat at the head of the table in a chair made heavy with decorations of gold and jewels, I say, "Tell me Ingemar, how did your reunion with your son go?"

I know very well how it went because of the cameras, but he doesn't need to know that. The two monsters that walked me in lift my chair with ease and bring it closer to the table before they go stand by the wall to wait for me. Ingemar grimaces into his food, "It went about as well as it could. He's figured out that I poisoned my late wife and he is none to happy about it. He will come around eventually. He just doesn't understand that sometimes things must be done."

Laughing, I tell him, "Indeed. And sometimes the things are murder. Don't worry, I understand. After all, my Conrí was one of the things that had to be done."

Ingemar lifts a shoulder briefly, "As it is, I think he will not be terribly cooperative until he gets over his current mood."

"Oh Ingemar, you still don't understand, do you? Pelos is here and alive for the sole purpose of controlling my daughter Eumeleia. As long as I have him in my possession, she will do whatever I tell her to do. Right now I could tell her to go murder a king in his sleep and she would give it her all in an attempt to get her Pelos back. He is nothing more than a tool. If he becomes useless, he will be discarded the same as would any other tool." I file away the fact that he kept hidden Pelos's news about who his father is. Assuming of course, that what Pelos said or what he was told, are both true.

Eumeleia

Storming away from the one person that could have my Pelos back today is probably one of the dumber things I have done recently. I know Valdís would do this for me if it is at all in her power. She has always been kind to me, no matter how awful I was to her.

This would all be so much easier if she had just done whatever mother wanted her to do. Or maybe died one of the times mother was trying to kill her. I wouldn't be dealing with any of this if only she could have just kept me out of it. But no. She couldn't just deal with whatever mother wanted of her, no, she had to be selfish.

She had to make it everyone else's problem instead of just hers. She could have worked with mother and found some way to make her happy if she had only tried. I know she could have, I kept mother plenty happy with me for all those years. It was easy!

But no, she couldn't do that. Couldn't let mother have the estate that should have been hers by right of survivorship. All because she worried about the damn peasants! Now I have to worry about what will happen to my Pelos. I am so deep in my thoughts I don't even notice the king in the hall I am walking through until I run into him. "Oh! Oh! I am so sorry! I wasn't paying attention, please forgive me!"

King Vincent grasps my shoulders to keep me stable as I am apologizing. He says, "I should have been watching as well. I was deep in my own thoughts. But you have been crying, why are you so upset? Was someone unkind to you?"

Hot tears roll down my cheeks at his kindness. I just want my Pelos. "It is nothing. Valdís sought me out and we had words. It's fine."

King Vincent scowls, "It is not fine. She sought you out to have harsh words with you even as you are trying to deal with the kidnapping of your husband? She is obviously a menace. I will have words with her and ensure this doesn't happen again while you are here with us. For now, you should go clean your face and lie down to rest until dinner."

I nod, "I do find that I am incredibly tired now. These dramatics of hers are draining. Thank you for listening, your highness." As I continue on down the hall I can't help but smile, knowing that Valdís is going to be punished for being mean to me. Everything feels a little more right with my world.

After seeing Vincent in the hall, I am much more at ease as I go to my room. A nap sounds nice, but I need to check my phone first. I see no one in the hall as I enter my room. After checking the entire room to ensure that no one else is in here I go directly to where I hid the phone. The chair next to the armoire is sturdy as I climb on it to reach the top. My phone is still there, resting where I left it.

A sigh of relief escapes me as I clutch it to my chest while I step down off the chair. This phone is my link to Pelos. Crossing the room I lock my door. I should have done that when I first entered. Stupid. I'll remember from now on.

Crossing to the bed and climbing on it, I make myself comfortable. Shoving pillows together up against the head-board to support my back and pulling the blankets around me. With everything as comforting as I can make it, I pull the phone away from my chest and hit the side button to light it up. A message! A few taps on the screen later and the phone is unlocked, revealing a message from the one number in this phone. It only says, "Call now."

Tapping the number I put the phone to my ear, listening as it rings. One, two, three, and halfway through the fourth ring a man answers, "Hello."

"I-I was told to call. This is Eumeleia."

"Yes. One moment."

Silence is a void I feel myself being sucked into when my mother says, "Eumeleia, so good to hear from you!"

"Yes Mother. I'm glad to hear your voice too. How are you?"

"I am doing well. Tell me about the kings. What are they doing?"

"I don't really know what they are doing Mother. I've barely seen them."

She sighs, "Eumeleia, I need you to see them. Insinuate yourself into their lives. Make them comfortable around you and listen. Men love to talk about themselves. A woman willing to listen to all their prattle makes their day."

"I will Mother. I just haven't been here very long. Three of them seemed to be very put off by the scent you asked me to wear. They were coughing and gagging."

"Ah, but two of them weren't? Which ones?"

"It was really only one, I haven't met the other. The one that was not put off by the scent is King Vincent."

She chuckles, "That is perfect. You put your focus on him. Be a friend to him. Get him to champion you and tell you all his worries.Create a divide between him and his brothers. This will help with your final task."

"What is my final task Mother?"

"Ah, don't you worry about that just yet. You do as you are told and I will expect daily reports on the kings and Valdís. What is she doing?"

"Right now King Vincent is probably yelling at her for bullying me. Beyond that, she seems to spend most of her time at a different castle, they are calling it the Witches Keep."

"Indeed. This would be the castle on the north end of Atlantis?"

"Yes, I think it is."

"Good. Keep collecting information for me Eumeleia. We will talk again tomorrow."

"Wait! Mother!"

"Yes, Eumeleia?"

"You have to let me speak to Pelos."

"Child, I am queen, I do not have to do anything."

"You're right. You don't have to do anything Mother. But if I don't speak to Pelos every day I will assume you have had him killed and therefore I will be throwing myself from the castle walls, sending all your plans straight to the trash. I know you had Conrí murdered and you tried to kill Valdís numerous times. I can't trust that you won't eliminate him just because you get annoyed with him. Or me."

She sighs, "Very well, since you are so very dramatic. Nicholas, take the phone down to Pelos."

I hear the man say "Yes, my queen."

* * *

Pelos

Times passes at a crawl when your life is restricted to a ten by ten cell. I have never in my life spent so much time staring up at a ceiling while laying on a single bed. I hear someone walking toward the room my cell is in and I look toward the door. Ah, Eirene's favorite bodyguard, Nicholas. I sit up as he approaches, "What can I do for the queen's favorite stooge?"

He scowls at me, "You have a call. Put this end," he points at the rectangle in his hand, "next to your ear. Speak normally and they will hear you."

I stand and step over to him as he passes the rectangle through the bars to me and I follow his directions, "Hello?"

"Pelos! Oh thank the goddess, you are still alive! I was so worried for you! Are you all right? Has she been treating you well?"

My knees go weak hearing her voice. Grabbing the bars to keep myself upright with one hand, "Oh Eumeleia, I thought I would never hear your voice again. Are you okay?"

"I'm fine. I am at the castle like mother wants, they are all being nice to me. But you are with my mother, is she feeding you? Do you have a clean place to sleep? Are you able to bathe?"

Of course she would be more concerned about my welfare. I don't deserve her. "Don't worry about me, I am fine. They have me in a good size cage, the room is temperature controlled, and they are feeding me. Yes, there is a bed, and I get to shower. You are who I am concerned about. If the kings find out what you are doing, they will kill you. Just go to them, tell them the truth and let what happens, happen. You need to just accept that I am going to die and go on with your life. I am happy that I was able to be a brief part of your life, I want you to be happy. And alive. Please, tell them the truth."

She shouts at me, "No! I won't do it! I can keep mother happy and keep you alive. You have got to stay alive for me, I can't go on without you. Pelos, don't you know I love you more than life itself? I told mother I would throw myself off the walls of the castle if I couldn't speak to you and verify that you live still. Please don't ask me to let you die. I can't do it."

"If you get the chance to save yourself, promise me you will. Eumeleia, I will die a happy man knowing I live on in your memories."

"I'm not sacrificing you for my freedom. You may as well accept that now. I'll talk to you again tomorrow. I love you, Pelos."

"I love you too, Eumeleia. Please, just let me die. I want you safe."

She ends the call in answer. Why won't she listen to reason dammit? She could live out the rest of her life safe if only she would let go of the hope that I will survive when we both know it is just a matter of time before Eirene kills me to teach Eumeleia some sick lesson.

A throat clears outside my cell and I turn to see

Nicholas still standing there. He extends his hand for the rectangle in my hand. As I pass it through the bars I tell him, "I meant every word I said. Eumeleia should just tell her mother to fuck off and let me die."

He is silent for a bit and then says, "There are worse things than death. You should take care that you don't let the wrong people hear you saying that."

Nine

Valdís

Today is the day.

We have a number of small groups that can connect to each other and I think it will be enough. It has to be enough. We have the courtyard shielded in pieces, one section of wall at a time, but it hasn't been supporting the walls as well as we had hoped. We feel certain that this is because the force isn't spread along the shields as a whole, they are all separate and varying strengths.

I watch each of the ten groups as they merge their powers. The joining of the magics creates a shield around the women joined, to me it looks like a dome of light around them. Once each group has lit up with the joining of power, the two most stable work to connect with each other. The groups all connect faster and smoother when I join in to connect them, but I worry that depending on me for this is going to come back to bite us all. They have to be able to function without me. What happens if I die? Or get kidnapped? It's happened before and it could happen again.

These women and what they pass on to the next generations of witches, they will be the best protection I can leave for my land. The final group connects and it is beautiful. The power flow is magnificent. Hours and hours of practice have paid off. "All right, you ladies are doing magnificent! Keep it smooth, group one, you take the lead and set the first layer." My heart swells with pride as the first layer goes without a hitch. "Group two, you're up!"

An hour later group ten is creating the final layer. I watch closely, I know all the women are tired from holding the connection so long. As the tenth layer goes into place I give the signal. Several other hidden witches start firing stunning shots at the group. The tenth layer wobbles, falters, and nearly disappears before they get it smoothed and lay it in place while under fire!

They get it set and I watch as they create a retaliatory pulse. I quickly throw up a shield so that they don't actually hit the women firing at them. Fuck, I didn't think it through. Shield up, I give the signal to the other women to cease fire. The women inside the shield send out their pulse and I feel it hit the shield I put up. It is a nice one. I can't help but jump and shout in joy at this amazingly fucking successful test! "Let go of the merge ladies, you did magnificent! I am so proud of each and every one of you!"

I walk overland spend time talking to the women who are tired but pleased with everything they accomplished today. Many of them talk about the surprise of the shots fired and I apologize to them, "I know that was really scary. But we needed to see that you all could hold it together even under attack. And look at what you all did! You held it together and created a counter attack that I was not prepared for, you all did so good."

Raising my voice so everyone can hear me I say, "Ladies!" Using my magic I float myself up so I can be seen by them too, "Ladies, I want you all to know that what you did here today was amazing. I am sorry to have frightened you, but I want to point out that you all didn't fold under pressure. And you prepared a counter attack on the fly that *I wasn't prepared for*. You all should be just as proud of yourselves as I am of you." The women cheer and I wait for them to quiet again, "Very soon I want us to practice opening portals and sending spells through them. And, we are going to keep practicing like this. The sad truth is, we need to expect an attack. It isn't a matter of if, it's when. From now on, the rule is, shields up. If you hear a weird thump at night, shields up. If you see something strange out of the corner of your eye, shields up. If you feel uneasy suddenly, shields up. War is coming and the monsters will be at our gates. Our land, our Goddess, will need us to fight and win. We cannot let the Outsiders take our families, our homes, and our powers from us. I don't want to lose a single one of you. So stay vigilant and practice!" The women shout their agreement and cheer as I lower myself back to the ground.

Making my way to the edge of the group I find Dagma waiting for me. She says, "Walk with me, please."

I nod and she slips her arm into mine, steering me toward the far side of the courtyard, "How long do you think we have?"

Shrugging, I tell her, "I don't know. I wish I did. I just feel that something big is coming. I know the Outsiders are not going to leave us alone. Now they even have more information about our land since they have Eirene. I think she might be royalty over there. Which potentially means that she will be spearheading the attack on our land."

Mom nods, "That surprises me not at all. How are you holding up?"

"I'm scared silly. I am terrified that they will kill our people. Sick with fear that my kings could be murdered in a senseless war because some asshole wants our Hekate's power. I'm near paralyzed with the idea that I could lose you or my grandmothers. The most terrifying part is that there is something in me saying, no, I am going to make sure none of that happens. If I have to take the life of every single Outsider, so be it. That I am so willing to kill them all kind of frightens me too. What if I am the evil in the world?"

Dagma stops mid-step and snatches me to facing her, she looks so angry. I don't think I have ever seen her look so pissed in all my life.

She practically growls out, "You have never been the evil in this world! How dare you think that! You insult me, your grandmothers, and Hekate with even entertaining such thoughts." She takes a breath and seems to calm a little, "My darling daughter, I'm sorry I was so forceful just then.

I feel quite strongly on the matter. Tell me, who has you thinking you are the evil in this world?"

My shoulders fall and I look away, "Eumeleia."

She carefully puts a finger on my chin and guides my face so that I am looking at her again, "Eumeleia is a brainwashed tool terrified of taking any responsibility for her actions. It is much easier to blame you for everything than to admit her mother is a greedy, conniving woman with no regard for anyone but herself."

"I know that, but sometimes I, it's just hard to remember."

She pulls me into a hug, "Then I'll just have to stick around and remind you, won't I?"

Vincent

I can't help but feel like poor Eumeleia has gotten a raw deal after our talk yesterday. Her mother took her husband because of this feud between her mother and stepsister. Now Valdís is bullying her when she is here for help. I need to talk to my brothers, they have got to do something about her. Obviously I can't say anything to her without losing my mind over her scent. It has to be them that speaks to her about this. With my mind made up, I start for Knox's office. We all use it, but for the most part, it is really his. The rest of us are interlopers completely uninterested in having an office. A pang of hunger runs through me, leaving me shaky and annoyed.

I can't fathom what the hell is causing this. I had food today. A large breakfast. I had blood today. Twice!

I never had this problem at the monastery. I ate like a normal vampire, sipping from people wandering the monastery at night once or twice a week since fresh is so much more filling than stored. Another pang rips through me just as the scent of Valdís reaches me. For one brief second everything eases, but then the burning comes back with a vengeance.

Damn her! She is walking into this hallway when she sees me, "Vincent, are you okay? Do you need help? Should I get one of your brothers?"

I growl out, "Am I ok? Why do you care? You certainly don't care about whether your sister is okay when you are busy bullying her." The shock on her face has my rage boiling over, "Did you think no one would find out? That you would just be able to bully her out of the castle and everything would be fine? How dare you!"

I didn't realize I had been stalking closer to her until she held a hand up in my face, "I don't know what is going on with you but I am not the one. I can arrange for you to take a swim right now if you can't cool yourself off."

What am I doing so close to her? Fuck, what is wrong with me? Stepping back from her I tell her, "You watch yourself with Eumeleia. I won't tolerate you bullying her. I will have you out if you can't contain your evil."

She laughs. This bitch is laughing at me as she says, "Oh, do you have shit wrong. Have a day Vincent. I'll send one of your brothers to check on you, you are not looking well at all and my presence seems to antagonize you."

I watch her as she continues on down the hall, walking away as though she hasn't a care in the world. As if she isn't leaving a vampire standing behind her. The urge to catch her and drain her is nearly overwhelming, my hands are shaking with it. One step at a time I force myself to turn away and walk the opposite direction.

What the fuck is wrong with me?

Ten

Valdís

This is my favorite time of the day. Today has been long, but good. We didn't lose any witches today and practice went really well. Now I am home and Chance is walking with me to my room. We all had dinner apart tonight so we could finish things. I hate it that we have to work so much right now but I understand that this is out of our control. Even with all that we are doing, it may not be enough.

I feel his arm slip around my waist as he says, "Was today one of the bad days?"

"Hm? Oh, no, not at all. Why?"

"Because you were frowning pretty fiercely at the hall carpet. Has it offended you? Shall we rip it out by the roots?"

I laugh, "Thank you for the offer, but no. The carpet is

fine. I was thinking about us not having dinner together today and that even with all we are doing, it still may not be enough. What if they attack us and we don't manage to fight them off? What if they overwhelm us and not even the combination of you all and me with my witches can stand against them?"

Chance tugs me to a stop and turns me to face him, "Then we die. My queen, it will be a battle. No matter how much we prepare, there are no guarantees in a battle. All we can do is our best and hope it is enough." He wraps his arms around me, his warm scent surrounding me and comforting me as he holds me close. "I love you Valdís. We love you. And we will do everything in our power to ensure that you survive, if we have to kill every damn one of them, that's what we'll do. We aren't the only ones that feel that way. Dagma is willing to murder the world if it will keep you safe. The two K's? They have been haunting Vincent since that last breakfast he was rude to you at."

"What? Mom nearly had a breakdown when she figured out that she could kill as well as heal. Haunting? I thought ghosts haunted people?"

I nearly jump out of my skin hearing Kalina speak from behind me, "Oh no sweet girl."

Chance holds me in place and backs himself against the wall, the shiver that went through him when they spoke was only noticeable because my hands were on him. Twisting around in the shelter of his arm I face them, "Fucking shit, are you trying to kill me?"

They giggle and Katerine says, "We would never. Besides, we would get Dagma here fast if you had a heart attack or something. We might even be able to slow it down. Probably wouldn't feel great but I think we could in a pinch."

Kalina nods, "And in answer to your questions, we can tell you that Dagma killed a great many people when they went to fetch you. She doesn't feel bad about it at all. As for the haunting, well, it is quite possible to haunt someone while you are still alive. Especially if the books Hekate gave you happen to have spells that are very useful in that way."

"I understand why you might be haunting him, what I don't understand is why you are here scaring the shit out of me?"

Katerine says, "Oh! Well, you see, Vincent often wanders over to the halls you generally take to your room about the time that you arrive home. Since he is often poorly behaved around you, we thought it might be easier to catch him at just the right time if we simply follow you."

Kalina giggles, "Besides, you lead a spicy life and those kings of yours are not hard on the eyes in any way. And your guards, goodness. You should see them around the barracks when they think no one is watching. So much man meat on display."

Chance's hold on me tightens a bit. I think I would not be allowed to leave him here alone with them under any circumstances now. "You can't sneak around and watch them when they think they are alone. It's not ok."

Kalina sighs, "I suppose pinching their cheeks is out of the question too?"

"Oh for fucks sake, tell me you haven't been pinching the guards cheeks without consent?"

Katerine's cheeks are suddenly rosy, "Not exactly? I mean, we did let them see us at that point so they don't think they were being haunted. That's a good thing, right?"

"No. I mean, yes, letting them see you is a good thing! You just can't go around pinching guards, oh sweet Lady, you weren't pinching their face cheeks were you?" They both look away, suddenly very interested in either end of the hall. Sighing from the bottom of my soul I tell them, "New rule. Old rule? Whatever. No touching anyone without invitation. Vocally articulated consent. And no peeping on people, that's just not ok. Not ok. I'm not ok after this conversation. Look at me," they turn innocent eyes on me, "I never once imagined that I would have Grandmothers and never in my wildest dreams did it occur to me that if I did, they might be salacious peeping Toms. It's fine if you want to watch over me and make sure Vincent doesn't catch me unawares. But no creeping. Hm. Yeah, you just have to do better." A brilliant idea occurs to me and I finish with, "Or, I will be forced to make it so that every time you see something you like, it suddenly looks like mudfish."

Their mouths fall open at the same time, "You wouldn't!"

"I would, if you can't respect them as people the way

you would want to be respected, then you will force me to do something to protect them the way you would me."

Katerine puts a hand over her mouth in horror as Kalina says, "Oh no. We didn't, I mean. We weren't seeing them as people. You're right. And now we are going to need to apologize to them. I suppose now is the best time."

Katerine is somewhat recovered and says, "Yes. We should find them now and apologize. We are truly sorry, we will do better. I guess we let the power go to our heads and ferment on some wrong ideas we had. Don't worry, we'll set it right and this will never happen again."

"Good. Thank you for being willing to listen. I'm sure I could have handled that better, I just—"

"Don't you worry about it." Kalina tells me, "We aren't the easiest of people to convince that something we have done might not be ok. We are just glad you took the time to make sure we understood. Now go, go get some rest. We love you, and we will refrain from hugging you tonight only because your Chance still looks quite uncomfortable. Sleep well darlings."

We both watch them leave, walking down the hall arm in arm. They look so sweet. So innocent. Looking back at Chance I ask, "Ready to get in my room and close the door?"

He nods, "Yes. Definitely yes. Maybe we could lock the door tonight?"

Chuckling, I pull away from him and start down the hall, "Possibly. But I am definitely making you answer the door."

"I feel like that is a fair trade for my peace of mind."

We make it to my bedroom without further incident. I takes me not long at all to get myself into the bed and Chance is there waiting, arms open for me. I am snuggled in with him, silent and mostly content when Knox knocks on the door and pokes his head in, "Space for me?"

"Of course, come in." He walks in, Malic and Gage arriving before he can close the door, he looks to me and I tell him, "Yes, them too. I'll take all the cuddles I can get. But make sure you lock the door behind you."

Malic frowns as he walks toward the bed, "What happened?"

"I would like to say that it was nothing more than the worries I have about the battle we all know is coming or the terrible things my grandmothers have been doing to the guards--"

Knox says, "What are they doing to them now? We might need them..."

Chance shakes his head, "Don't ask. She took care of it. Let's just leave it at only one of us having those nightmares."

Gage laughs, "Done. I don't want to know."

Malic's frown deepens, "Chance, I expect a full report tomorrow. I need to know about anything that might affect their ability to fight. For now, what is bothering you Valdís, would it have anything to do with you sending one of the butlers to find me and advise that I check on Vincent?"

Chance says, "You didn't mention that earlier!"

Shrugging, I tell him, "We got interrupted by my

Grandmothers. That took precedence over my run in with Vincent."

Gage's frown matches Malic's as he says, "He smells sick, I like it not that he is free to roam unchecked. It isn't safe for you."

Knox sits heavily, "We can't imprison him."

"We can't and we shouldn't. It's no crime to be sick and it isn't like I can't defend myself. Honestly, I have no problem with setting him on fire should he try to bite me. More importantly, I am generally shielded. My shields won't protect me from my own clumsiness, but he isn't going to be able to tear me into pieces or something. The stronger the force that hits me the more magic pours into protecting me. If someone tries to stab me, at most I will get a shallow cut."

Malic nods, "That does give me some reassurance. Now what did he do?"

Sighing, I tell him the whole story. Except the part where he called me evil. That still hurts my heart and I don't want them to hate Vincent. If he really is sick somehow, and anything is possible, it would be too cruel to take his brothers from him over me. And what if he is right? What if I am the evil?

Knox shakes his head, "I just can't understand how he can even manage to breathe in her presence. She is wearing some awful perfume, it smells of decay and rot. It was difficult to hold my revulsion the one time I was in the same room as her. He says that he finds the scent calming. If that isn't a sign of illness, I don't know what is."

Gage nods, "She leaves a trail of rot everywhere she goes. The castle smells foul. I don't know why she is here, but I would feel better if she wasn't." His opinion shared he pulls his shirt over his head and drops it to the floor. One tug on the ties at his waist and his pants drop to the floor as he shifts into his beautiful wolf form.

I immediately roll over so my back is snuggled against Chance and pat the bed in front of me. Gage jumps onto the bed, walking across to me. He flops down heavily, his weight pushing me further into Chance.

Malic asks, "How is it even possible that Vincent is falling for this shit?"

Knox says, "I don't know. What I do know is that I am not spending the night sneezing with your fucking fur shedding all over the damn place, Gage. You sleep against her ass. Or we could shave you?"

Gage sits up and growls at him while I laugh. I feel Chance's chest shake with repressed laughter. "Here Gage," I say as I roll onto my back and spread my legs under the blanket, "You can lay here." I swear he looks smug as he stands, walks over and very gently lays down between my legs. He is very careful as he rests his massive head on my belly.

Malic shakes his head, "Good job Knox." Then he dives across the bed, landing in the spot so recently vacated by Gage.

Knox laughs, "That's fine, I can cuddle up to you Malic, it's the fur I find objectionable."

Gage shifts forms, "I got the better spot, fur or no. And she pets me whether or not I have fur so it's fine."

As he says that I realize I still have my hand on his head, scratching gently like I was while he was in wolf form. Chuckling I say, "Knox, turn off the light and come to bed."

Eleven

V incent

The hunger just won't abate today. My hands are shaking with it and I am angry at every little sound. Even the feel of my clothing against my body is scratchy and aggravating. I want to tear the world down around me, but I know that isn't reasonable. I don't know what is wrong with me and it scares me that I feel so violent about everything.

It scares the hell out of me that it feels like my body is eating itself all the time. I thought when Hekate made us vampires that we wouldn't feel these things ever. Did she take it away from me? Or part of it? Would she do that?

Pacing here in the garden isn't going to answer my questions, but I can't call her. Hekate hasn't spoken to any of us in years. I know she isn't going to be willing to speak to me just because I have a problem. And what if it is my fault? What if something I did fucked it all up and I am just this broken, useless creature? Would she put me out of my misery? Do I want her to?

I pick up the sound of two people walking this way. I think about hiding but the anger rises in me for even thinking about that and I plant my feet, facing in the direction the sounds are coming from. Soon enough those two old ladies, staunch supporters of that damned Valdís, round the corner and smile when they see me, saying, "King Vincent, good morning! How are you this fine day?"

"What are you doing out here?"

They had kept walking but now they turn as a unit to face me, "We are tending the gardens. It is what we are best at and the garden does bring our Valdís such pleasure."

Snarling at them I say, "There is no need for your tending them, we have gardeners for this. This is what the fuck we pay them for."

The smiles never leave their faces as they take a step toward me, "Why exactly are you trying so hard to be mean to us?"

"Because you belong in a home! Not wandering my gardens and disturbing my peace!"

Their smiles are getting creepy now as they seem to grow wider, "You want us out of your gardens and out of your peace, yet you detained us. Do you see the problem there?"

Narrowing my eyes at their tone, "Are you fucking kidding me? I should have you put in a home myself! You two are a bloody menace and shouldn't be walking around disturbing everyone."

One of them says, "Define everyone. No one else has voiced a complaint. In fact, the other kings are quite nice to us."

My eyes roll of their own volition, "That's because they are scared of you. I don't know what you did to them, but it's not going to work on me!" Just as they start to laugh the vines clamp down on my legs. I try to tear them away, but more grow to take their place as fast as I can tear them away. Even as I work to free my legs, the vines grow past my hands and up my thighs. Within seconds my arms are pinned to my sides. I am trapped and only now realizing that I never had a chance against their magic. I glare at the two old women, "You let me out of here! Right now!"

They have the nerve to laugh at me as they walk away. One says over her shoulder, "Don't worry! I'm sure someone will be around sooner or later."

I'm going to murder a couple of old women. They are going to call me a killer of Grannies and I won't care. Those two deserve it! How dare they! "Guards!"

Valdís

"I really don't think we should be walking out here right now, Gage. I stopped coming out here in the mornings because he is usually out here."

His lip curls, "And that is why we are out here. You are not giving up something you love because my brother is not well. If I have to walk with you every morning, then that is what I will do." He steps in front of me, putting his hands on my shoulders, "Valdís, you have given up too much for the comfort of others and because you had no choice. It is in my power to make sure you still have this pleasure in your life. My brother will simply have to deal with it or we can fight like we used to, either way is fine with me. But you, you are going to wander the gardens and enjoy."

Sighing, I tell him, "I'll try but the fact is, I can smell Vincent here. He is definitely ahead of us and I am not unaffected. Are you sure we can't just turn around and not bother him?"

"I am. And I was content to pretend you were affected by me." And then he steps to the side as he turns to face forward, putting an arm around me and firmly guiding me forward.

"Well, yes, I am but—"

"Guards!"

Gage and I look at each other when we hear Vincent shouting for guards. I shield us both as we run toward the sound. Gage skids to a stop in front of me and I hit his back because I can't stop that fast. He reaches back to steady me with one arm as I peer around him to see why he stopped. Holy shit. This has to have been the two K's. Oh no. He looks furious. I know my mouth is hanging open and I am staring, but he is covered in vines up to his chin. Gage chuckles and I look up at him, "You're going to antagonize him!"

He laughs, "I don't know if you noticed, but he looks pretty thoroughly antagonized already. My laugh might add to it but mostly he is going to be mad no matter what right now." He walks over to Vincent, "So, um, is this a new kink or did you piss off one of the witches?"

Vincent grinds out, "No, this is not some new kink! What is wrong with you?"

Gage smiles and crosses his arms in front of his chest, "There may be things wrong with me but I would like to point out that I am not stuck in the garden with living vines holding me in place."

"You are pushing it, Gage. There is only so much I am willing to take from you."

"Oh? Should I call Chance out? He really is much better at the sarcastic remarks than I am, perhaps you just want a pro?"

"What I want is for you to get me out of this, *right now*!"

Gage looks to me and I shake my head no. There is not a chance that he will be able to remove the vines from Vincent's body. "Sorry to tell you brother, but we are going to have to let Valdís get these vines off of you."

"I don't want her anywhere near me. What is it? Are you just too weak to tear away the vines?"

"Vincent, you may want to stop being such a jackass while you are already being taught a lesson by someone else. I may decide you need more time in there."

"Dammit all Gage! Just get me out of here, I don't care if you have to convince the evil bi—"

Crack

Vincent's head jerks with the slap Gage delivered. I

can't hear what he is saying to Vincent but there is hair sprouting on Gage in various places and his ears are looking pointy. When he leans back he shakes his head and with everything now appearing to be all man again, I venture to ask him, "Gage, is everything good?"

He nods, "Yes, it was just that both of us were offended. Can you get my brothers out here before we set him free?"

"Of course, one moment." I turn away from them and close my eyes a moment to feel where they are, happily, they are just breaking up from a morning meeting in Knox's office. I walk a little ways away from them down the path, opening a portal into his office and stepping through, "Gentlemen, your presence is requested in the gardens." They all look at me with questions in their eyes and I hold up my hand with the palm facing toward them, "It will be easier to just show you."

Knox shrugs and I turn to step back through the portal. The three of them are on my heels as I step back into the gardens, I can hear Gage and Vincent talking though not clearly enough to understand. They stop speaking as we walk up and both men look at us, both angry. "Are we interrupting? We can go back through the portal, I haven't closed it yet."

Gage shakes his head no, "Come on over, we need to get him out of this so we can continue our conversation."

"We are done talking. Set me free so I can go find those old women!"

I take the opportunity of him bitching at his brothers to really study him. I didn't realize how hollow his cheeks were. Is it normal for vampires to have dark shadows under their eyes? Malic almost died from the poison festering in his chest and he looked fine until he was nearly dead on my bedroom floor.

Vincent can't be okay. My heart clenches at the thought of how much he must be suffering even as my mind reminds me that he would like to go kill my grandmothers in a very violent manner right now.

The longer I watch him the more I can see the evidence of his decline. The little tension lines around his eyes and pupils much too big for the amount of light here. The way his jaw is tight, even when he speaks. I have to go find and talk to my mom. He needs to be scanned as soon as she can possibly get around him to do it surreptitiously.

Of course, I'll have to make sure the two K's are safe first. Turning away from my kings I cast a quick spell to figure out where my grandmothers are right now and a second one to close the other portal. Oh good, they are at the Witches Keep. I open a portal to my bedroom there before turning to my kings again, "Gentlemen," and they don't hear me. Ok, one magically augmented clap coming right up. I clap and the magic I wove into the clap makes it sound like thunder rolling right here. It is so loud it hurts my ears a little. It worked though. They aren't talking anymore and I have their full attention. "Gentlemen, I do need to get to the Keep today. To that end, I am containing Vincent in a box, and releasing his bonds." My hands move fast as I talk, carrying out what I said would happen. "Vincent will be released from the box in fifteen minutes. I would appreciate it if you could keep him away from the keep and I will keep the two K's at the keep for at least today."

Malic nods, "We can do that. You be safe, Knox, go with her."

Knox grins and says, "My pleasure. I so rarely get to play guard and I really prefer it. Say, is that your bedroom? I have another version of guard we could play in there if you are up for it."

I can't help but to laugh at his suggestion, "Sorry, I have work to do. Come on, I want to be gone long before the shield releases him."

* * *

Chance

As soon as the portal closes behind them Malic asks, "How did you piss them off enough to leave you here like this?"

He snarls at us as he tests the boundaries of his temporary prison, "I was here minding my own business when they came and accosted me."

I can't keep from mentioning, "You know, I have run into them numerous times and been found by them in the garden. A few of those times while I was railing their granddaughter. Not once, for all my sarcasm and mouthy ways did they get to the point of using their magic on me. Make me wildly uncomfortable? Yes. Hands down I have never been so uncomfortable as when those two dirty old women saw me naked. All that to say, I call bullshit. What did you do?"

All three of them are standing there staring at me. Malic says, "They saw you naked?"

"Every inch as Valdís immediately ran for her clothing."

Gage rolls his shoulders, the grimace on his face making him look like he is in pain. Malic shivers, turning to focus on Vincent, "Now that I have a new fear unlocked, what did you do?"

Vincent crosses his arms over his chest, turning his attention to something on the ground, "I might have been annoyed when they interrupted my alone time with their greeting and said something to the effect of they needed to be in a home."

Malic groans, running a hand across the back of his neck, "Vincent. Really? I know you are having problems, but you can't go after the witches here. It isn't safe. Even when we had witches before, we didn't have so many and they sure as shit weren't banding together. Please, do not antagonize the witches. We are going to need you and I am not sure exactly what these women can do, how far they can go. I do know that Dagma can kill people without ever touching them. I don't think that is limited to just humans."

Vincent seems surprised, "Really? You think she could take us out?"

Malic says, "I don't think she would even break a sweat to do it. She doesn't want to, but if you hurt her mother or aunt, or Goddess forbid, her daughter, I don't think there is a power on earth that would save the person responsible."

Gage nods, "He's right. You weren't here when we fetched Valdís back. I don't know how necessary we really were."

Vincent asks, "How many were there?"

I tell him, "Roughly a couple hundred. She walked through with a witch holding a shield and men fell left and right. It's possible she could be overwhelmed, if it was her alone. But we don't know that she can't decide to take out large swathes of people at a go if she chose. Personally, I don't want to test the theory."

Vincent says, "I see. Perhaps I could agree that I was rather harsh with them and they're not really acting out of turn."

Malic sighs in relief, his shoulders dropping a bit with the release of tension, "I am glad to hear you choose that. Come, let us go to our work for the day."

Twelve

Valdís

Closing the portal behind us with a wave of my hand, I keep walking straight through to the door. The two K's are in the courtyard and that is where I need to be. Knox is right beside me as I stride through the keep. At some point he takes my hand, holding it as he easily keeps up with me. It feels good, comforting, to have him on my side like this. To have them.

Before, it was Dagma, Quorin, Lommán, and I trying to work together to keep out of sight of my mother, all of us just trying to stay alive. Now I have four kings at my back and a small army of powerful women along with my own power to protect my family and my people. And that is what I am going to do, even if I have to protect them from a king that makes my blood boil with rage and my body weak with lust. We reach the courtyard and find the two K's working with Dagma to teach some of the newer witches. "Dagma, could you call a break for the class? I need to talk to Kalina and Katerine, I feel like you should be there too."

Mom looks at me, question in her eyes but she turns back to the class, "All right, you heard her. Let's break for an hour and we'll see you back out here then."

The women release whatever they had been working on and start clearing out. Most of them still look a little shell shocked. They all look that way the first week or so, I wonder if I looked that way the first week? The two K's look very innocent as they walk over, Dagma is smiling at me like I hung the moon. I am so glad she is really my mom, I don't know what I would have done without her all that time.

"So, does anyone want to tell me how King Vincent ended up wrapped in vines in the garden?"

The two K's smile widely, "We do!" Once they explain to us what actually happened, I feel like they were somewhat justified. Knox has to walk away, he is trying not to laugh and failing miserably. Dagma has covered her face with a hand and I am almost certain that she is laughing.

"I understand why you did that. And I can't even say you shouldn't do that again. Maybe he will learn a lesson from this. But, and this is why I wanted you here Mom, we think Vincent is sick. He doesn't seem healthy the way a vampire should. He has stress lines on his face and his pupils are dilated, even in the sunlight."

Dagma frowns, "That shouldn't be happening, human or vampire."

Knox, back with his composure says, "And, as hard as it may be to believe, his behavior is changed. The Vincent you have seen is not the Vincent we know. He was smart and quick and caring. Kind even. We all have had some changes happen from waiting so long and having certain memories hidden from us, but nothing like what Vincent is displaying now."

Dagma nods, "I will scan him as soon as possible. I am guessing you all would prefer the initial scan be done without his knowledge?"

Knox nods, "I think it would be best. I don't want to make him feel so heavily scrutinized if there is nothing wrong with him. Maybe he changed while he was gone. It's possible, but I hope this isn't who he is now."

Dagma shrugs, "I will scan him as soon as I can. In the meantime, you will make sure that Valdís is kept safe from him."

Knox shakes his head in a vigorous yes motion, "Absolutely! We want her safe the same as you do."

* * *

Eirene

"Nicholas, have the Cardinals brought out. Clean them up and bring them to my map room. The day is coming when we attack Atlantis, I want them helping as they should. If they don't, well, we'll feed them to my monsters."

I see him in my mirror as he shivers at the last bit, "Yes your highness, I'll see that it is done."

"Thank you Nicholas, you are so good to me." He has his phone out and is already messaging someone to tend to the cardinals even as I thank him. I finish adding some touches to my makeup for the day. I want to make sure I look suitably powerful when the cardinals see me again.

Coming out of my bathroom and into my bedroom, I find my dress for the day laying on the bed. Nicholas always blushes and turns away when I walk about under-dressed as he calls it, today is no exception. Perhaps I will take him as a lover for a time.

For now, I slip the dress on and turn to him, "Nicholas, could you come zip me up? These long zippers are such a trial."

He says something that comes out in a garbled croak, clears his throat and manages, "Yes, your majesty."

I feel the heat of him behind me as he near whispers, "I am going to touch you now, your majesty."

"Please do, Nicholas," I tell him, smiling. I know he can't see me smiling but I can feel his careful, hesitant movements as he works to zip my dress up without revealing more of my ass than what he can already see. The zipper moves upward so slow it seems to take an eternity. Then, suddenly it is done. He exhales shakily as he steps away.

Such a sweet man. I look forward to corrupting him. "Come, take my arm and let's go to the map room."

He is such a confident man where security and tactical missions are concerned. Now that a queen flirts with him in private, he is a blushing innocent. His body trembles from the contact with mine as we walk. He releases my arm like it was burning him as soon as we arrive in the map room. I go directly to the map of Atlantis that I brought with me when I left that shitty place. The castles are marked well on this map, with new notes denoting which is the castle they spend the most time in and which is the place where the witches hide. I look up from the map to find Ingemar, Kleitos, and the Cardinals have all joined me and stood waiting like the good boys I knew they could be. Four of my monsters have joined us as well, I look to the lead monster, "You, come and be part of this. You will need to know the plan," then I look to the cardinals. "Gentle cardinals, how are you today? I am sure you have not enjoyed your sojourn in my dungeons, but it would appear that you begin to understand your position. Do you find that assessment correct?"

They all look to Cardinal Abel. So he is the ringleader. Good. I know who to have killed if they won't behave. Cardinal Abel finds my eyes on him and quickly nods, "Yes, um, yes your highness. We fully understand our position. We appreciate your graciousness in allowing us out of the dungeons."

One of the cardinals smirks and scoffs. I ask him, "Cardinal Callusus, care to share with us all why you are making those noises?"

He looks up at me with defiance in his eyes. One of the monsters leaves the wall and begins to edge his way around the room as Cardinal Callusus says, "I am ashamed that Cardinal Abel caved simply for being held in a dungeon for a period of time. You are nothing to us and our God will tear you apart."

I laugh, "Oh, you think he will? Fool! It was his idea to send you to the dungeons!" Cardinal Callusus is just about to say more when the monster grabs him from behind, a hand going over his mouth to silence his screams. The monster takes him out of the room and off somewhere else. I don't know if he will eat him or perhaps pass him off to one of the others, but I don't care either. I look at the ones left, "Does anyone else feel as ex-Cardinal Callusus did?" Cardinal Abel shakes his head no quite vigorously, as do the rest of them. It would seem their rebellion is fully at an end. "Good, now that's taken care of, Cardinal Abel, you may stand over here and communicate any knowledge you or your brethren may have that would be useful to my plan to take Atlantis. If it isn't helpful, keep it quiet."

Now that he has his instructions I hear him and the remaining cardinals talking amongst themselves before Cardinal Abel walks over to look down at the map on the table. I look to the monster on my right, "What are you called?"

He looks at me like I have grown another head, "What?"

"Name. You have a name, yes?"

"I do, but only the other monsters have ever used it."

"Why?" I don't want to insist he tell me if this is some law that our God lay down for them.

He shrugs, "No one asked before. The few that spoke to us just called us monster."

"Is it something I can pronounce?" He nods and I say, "Then tell me. I would have your name."

He sighs, "My name is Gus."

"Well, Gus, let's plan a war."

Thirteen

P elos

These daily conversations with my Eumeleia are the only thing that keep me going. I beg her every day to just tell the kings what is going on. Today is no different as I tell her, "Love, the kings have the witches now. I feel certain they could help us if you are so determined that I live through this. Please, tell them."

I can almost see her shaking her head no, "Pelos, you don't understand. Valdís hates me. She has most of the kings turned against me already. If I reveal that I was sent here, by my mother, she will ensure that they have me killed. I just know it."

"If that is the case then we will meet in the afterlife and seek better roles in the next life. I will find you Eumeleia, that I promise."

She sighs, I know she is tired of hearing the same arguments from me. "I want you alive in this lifetime. Trust me.

I will keep you alive and I will make sure we are together again. Mother didn't set all this in motion because she intends to keep me in the castle for months on end. I promise, we will be together soon."

"Eumeleia, you know I can't deny you anything, I will do as you wish. Just, promise me that you'll let me go if you can't see a way to save us both."

"I can't promise that, Pelos. I would die with you first. I love you, and I have to go. We'll talk tomorrow."

"I love you."

I feel bereft when the device goes silent.

Ingemar

Foolish boy. He's got it bad for that twit Eumeleia. It's like he never even considered hiding his devotion to her. I watch him stare at the phone, long after the call has ended. "Pelos, she will call again tomorrow. Staring at the phone will not change things. Man up already."

His eyes narrow even as he presses his lips together, "Did you ever even care for her a little? Was your heart always just a collection of broken glass? Is that why you can't stand to see anyone show emotion? Or is it that you never had any ability to feel anything?" He puts an arm through the bars and tosses the phone at me, "I am glad that I can disappoint you in this way, Father. The fact of the matter is, I love Eumeleia beyond all reason. I beg her nightly to let me die so she can be free and live a good life."

He is such a disgrace. Tears running unchecked down his face, what if someone sees? "Pelos, get yourself together. You will live exactly as long as you are useful. You may want to think about how you can be more useful here. Then, if Eumeleia gets brought here, you can be a worthy companion for her. You won't be able to be much more than a companion for her, she will need to continue the royal line. But better that than nothing at all, eh?"

His lip curls in disgust, "I hope I get to see it when you die and I hope it hurts the whole fucking time. I hope my mother gets to see it from wherever she may be now. Now that she isn't suffering because the shit husband that couldn't love her or even please her had to kill her to keep his own insecurities at bay. Get out. I'm done talking to trash for the night."

With a sigh I turn and head for my room, stopping along the way to give the phone to a guard. The boy just has no survival instincts. Here I am, a stranger in a land that wants everyone from my land dead and I walk freely in the palace while most of my companions still rot in a cell. Kleitos, he walks free for the moment but I think his time here is growing short as he annoys Eirene further. Now my boy is so stuck in his feelings that he can't see his way to survival and I just don't know how to get through to him. It will be a shame to watch him die.

Fourteen

V aldís

This chair sucks. But the two K's love the view from this room and I am certainly not going to let them sit in the chair that hurts me. We are taking a break from teaching today, and from fetching more witches. But, we are not idle for all that we are sitting in a room with a view. Nope. We are chopping up herbs and tree bits. Because, as they keep reminding me, we must be able to tend to our hurts early, before they become something serious.

I don't disagree, I just want to go lay in the sun in the garden. Maybe it will still be bright when we— or not. Dark clouds are rolling in, I can see a line of rain moving this way. Oh well, I guess it will be a little easier to stay inside and do this now.

Tuning back into the conversation I listen as Kalina says that the herb she is so carefully laying out to dry one plucked leaf at a time will help the women of our land with cramps, but the bark I am shaving will do more for the ones that have it bad. Dagma sighs, "Only if we can make it taste better. There has to be a way to make this stuff more palatable."

The two K's cackle, with Kalina saying, "Oh there's plenty of ways. We just didn't share it with you a second time after you didn't listen the first time."

Dagma says, "What? Mother! How could you?"

Katerine laughs, "Easily. It isn't like we hid the information from you. We simply decided that we would not mention it again until you did. We had no idea it would take fifty years."

I can't help but laugh at mom's face. "Shit!" I drop the knife to one side and the piece of wood I was working on the other; putting pressure on my thumb to slow down the bleeding. And fuck, it is bleeding profusely. Standing, I start across the room, telling them, "I'll be back, I need to grab a cloth to soak this up with before I get it everywhere."

Dagma stops me halfway across, saying, "Wait, let me heal it and then you can just go clean up. No worry about bleeding everywhere."

"Oh, sur—" I am cut off by a roar. My eyes widen as I turn to the door and see a blur that kinda looks like Vincent coming at me. "Oh fuck!" I throw my hands up to cast something, anything, at him to stop him. Blood flies everywhere. I manage to throw ice at him and stop him running just barely an arms length away, he reaches for me and I fall back trying to get away from him, hitting the floor hard. He is snarling and trying to break the ice away from his legs.

Holy fuck, my thumb is still bleeding all over as I try to get my wits together enough to cast something that will contain him. Fuck it, more ice it is, maybe it will cool him down because I can't think of anything else right now. I get him frozen in place from the elbows down and flop back on the floor, Dagma is at my side. I didn't even notice her arrival on the floor next to me. But now I can see her face. She is mad. "It's ok. I'm ok Mom! Really, He didn't touch me, see? Look at me Mom, please! Mom, you can't kill the king. Please! Mom, help me."

That finally gets her to look at me, she sees me still holding my thumb and almost seems to come out of a trance, "Oh honey, I'm so sorry. Let me take care of that for you." She takes my hand in hers and I can almost feel the skin knitting itself back together. This is not the most pleasant feeling I have ever had. But it is bearable and she is focused on healing me, not murdering a king, so I'll take it.

She finishes the healing and I ask her, "Could you scan him now? I think this may be the best time, since whatever is affecting his behavior is fully in control right now."

Dagma nods, "I think I need a minute more before I can safely do that, but I will. Can we make him quiet? The shouting isn't helping."

"Yes we can. In fact, I am happy to do it." Mom could have done this better, but she is in no condition yet. So I cast a small, soundproof bubble around his head. He can scream till his vocal cords give out, we won't hear a thing though he could still hear us, if he stopped shouting.

She stands and reaches a hand down to me, I accept it

gratefully and stand, pulling her into a hug. I know a lot of the times when I almost died she just needed to hug me for a while and I suspect that this may feel like one of those to her. She hugs me tight for a bit and when she pulls away, her eyes are a little misty. "I promise, I'm ok Mom."

"I know, I know. It just shook me. I can, I can scan him now." She looks at him, "Oh my, he is still yelling, isn't he?"

"Eh, yeah. He seems pretty caught up."

I watch her walking around him, studying him closely.

Malic

We are going over the charters for the umpteenth time when Gage lifts his head, "Do you smell that?" No sooner than he asks he takes off at a run. Knox and I jog to follow him. Chance spots us and catches up, "Why are we running?"

That's when we smell it. Her blood. Valdís's blood on the air here in the castle, "Oh fuck!" We all speed up, Gage isn't far ahead of us when he stops at a door. We all skid to a stop next to him. Dagma is walking around Vincent who is encased in ice from the elbows down. He is struggling and appears to be shouting at Dagma, though its like the sound is turned off somehow. The scent of Valdís's blood permeates the air here. It is splashed about and there is more than a little on her. The two K's look shaken as they hold each other and watch. Valdís spots us and walks over, Vincent tracks her movements. She keeps her voice low, "Maybe wait out here until Dagma is done? She's not feeling very charitable toward him right now and I'm not sure how far that will extend."

Gage nods, "Are you ok? Why is your blood spilled?"

She waves a bloody hand at us, "I cut my thumb. That's all. Vincent never touched me. Not that he wasn't trying and scary as hell. But he never got to touch me."

My shoulders slump as I exhale, "Thank Goddess, I think I can speak for every one of us when I say that smelling your blood on the air scared the hell out of all of us." My brothers nod in agreement, "Do you think she might be willing to allow us in the room now, she is just staring at him."

Valdís turns, "Yeah, a little more distraction might be a good thing now."

I walk in and stop a short distance from Dagma, I do not want her to feel threatened by me. "Do you have any idea what is happening to him?"

She nods, "I do. But I don't understand it. You all can't do drugs, right?"

I shrug, "I guess we could, it just isn't ever really going to do anything for us."

Dagma nods, "That's what I thought, but I would swear he is dealing with withdrawals. That's what this reads as and I don't understand it at all. Whatever, or whoever, he was eating before he came home, we don't have it here and there was something in it to which he has become fully addicted."

Valdís asks, "Would my blood help? He seems to be

heavily fucked up over it, maybe he craves it because whatever he was drinking out there smells like my blood?"

"No! You are not letting him drink from you in this state! That is out of the question! What are you thinking!"

When she narrows her eyes and puts her hands on her hips, I know I have just made a big mistake. She says, "You listen good, Malic. You will not be telling me what I can or cannot do. And if you want to argue with me about this, I am going to suspend you up around the ceiling till I finish and you can have your own damn soundproof bubble to match his!" She points at Vincent and I realize why we can't hear him even though he is obviously shouting his head off.

Think fast Malic, say something good to keep her from hanging you like a damn light fixture, "I am very sorry. I was not thinking, I just don't want you to be injured with him as out of control as he is right now."

She seems mollified as she turns her attention away from me to her mother. Dagma has a little smirk on her face as she says, "I honestly cannot be sure. Possibly? Maybe we should ask Hekate?"

Fifteen

Valdís

Calling Hekate has only gotten easier. I don't even need the candles anymore. A few calming breaths and whispering her name does it. It feels like coming home. Opening my eyes with a sigh of contentment, I see her, right in front of me. She is smiling softly at me, "You are doing so good Valdís. I am proud of you. What do you need?"

I half turn and point at Vincent, still thoroughly trapped, "There is something wrong with him. Mom says that she would swear he is having withdrawals? As if he had been addicted to something. We don't understand how that is possible. But, um, he tried to attack me while my thumb was bleeding."

She looks at him, the silence in the room is heavy as we, or at least I, try to not even breathe as she studies him. Hekate breaks the silence saying, "Oh Vincent, how did you think you could stay at one of his monasteries and not be immediately known for who and what you are?" She looks so sad as she waves a hand at him. "I have made it so that he cannot hear us and so that your stepsister has forgotten everything she heard from the time my name was first mentioned. She was hovering in the hall but now believes that you all have left the room. She is on her way to hers and will hear no more of our conversation. As for Vincent, your blood will cure him. It will burn the taint of what he was fed out of him."

"What, um, what was he fed?"

"Monsters. He was fed on their monsters the entire time he was there. Their blood, over time, is addictive. I don't think their god thought that through, but my concern is only that you all," she looks at my kings, "do not drink often from the monsters. During a couple battles, while fighting, it will be fine. Especially if you sip from her," she gestures at me, "within the next few days after. A week, two, of feeding from them and you will be just as addicted as he is right now."

Knox, looking at Vincent and myself, says, "Won't he try to drain her completely?"

Hekate nods, "He will, but as soon as her blood hits his system, it is going to feel like he has been set on fire from the inside. He isn't going to be able to keep drinking."

I turn around and really look at Vincent. The stress lines on his face, the tightness in his eyes. The sparseness of his frame. He looks like he has been wasting away. He sees me staring and he snarls at me, I can't hear him, but I watch his lip curl. I see the disgust in his eyes. Is this going to help? Will he hate me more? Be forever convinced that I am the evil in this world? He turns his face from me and his eyes fall on Malic. His shoulders drop, just fractionally and for one brief second I see the pain on his face.

Squaring my shoulders and taking a deep breath, I walk over to him. He looks at me with a deep hunger in his eyes. Swallowing, I lift a wrist up till it is even with his mouth and slowly, I force myself to move it toward him. I just know it's gonna hurt when he bites me. His teeth break my skin as he clamps down on my wrist, oh fuck, it definitely hurts. Biting my lip, I focus on not making a noise that might drive Dagma to drastic measures. It feels like he is trying to bite through my arm, bone and all. The pressure is beyond intense until suddenly, it's gone. I look at his face, it is contorted in pain. I look to Hekate as I pull my injured wrist in to cradle it against my body.

She looks so sad as she says, "Let your mother heal you again. He hurts right now, but it will pass."

Dagma is in front of me then, her back to Vincent and urging me toward a chair. I sit in the chair she guides me to, I kind of love being tended by her. Admittedly, I would prefer to not feel like something was trying to crunch through my bones. When she pulls my arm away from my body, ever so gently, it still hurts like hell. Her eyes flash with an inner fire as she assesses the damage done. She is so gentle as she works to heal my arm, it is no less uncomfortable than a little while ago when she healed my thumb, only this seems a lot deeper.

Vincent is still thrashing, as much as he can in his icy prison. I hate seeing it, even if he isn't my friend. I look to Hekate, "Isn't there anything that can be done for him? Can't we knock him out or something?"

She frowns and shakes her head no, "If we ease it, in any way, it will allow some of the taint left by years of drinking their blood to remain. He will still crave their blood and yours. You would not be safe around him. We have to let it burn out of him completely."

* * *

Eumeleia

I can't help but dread these calls as much as I look forward to them. Mother presses me hard for information that I don't have to give. Information that I can't get without getting close to a king in ways that I just can't do. King Vincent is nice, and I think I could be his friend, but I cannot get close enough to him in this short time without breaking the vows between Pelos and I. That's just not something I will ever do.

Pacing the room, phone held to me like it might run away, I try to think of anything I have heard today that she might be interested in. The nausea makes it hard to think, but I have to find something. It finally hits me what I should tell her and I lift the phone away from my body and touch the buttons to start the call. A man answers, "Hello."

"Let me speak to my mother, now." My knees quake as I say that but I manage to keep my voice steady.

Much faster than any time before, my mother answers, "Hello, Eumeleia. What news have you got for me?"

"King Vincent is fully against Valdís. He attacked her today, in full sight of everyone. He was stopped before she was injured much, but there was a lot of blood."

"Really? And what are the other kings saying?"

"There seems to be dissent between them. The other kings are not happy with him at all."

I can almost see the cruel smile form on her face as she says, "The timing for this couldn't be better. Your time in the castle is nearly done. In four days days you are going to cause a scene. Your task will be to keep as much of the castle busy as you possibly can, at the very least, the kings and Valdís. Maybe arrange for him to attack her again, only with more success? Whatever you decide, you just make sure they stay distracted for at least two hours."

"Two hours? I don't know if I can do that, Mother."

"You had best find a way to do that if you want your precious Pelos to stay alive. All it will take is a phone call and he will be gone. Forever."

My heart drops somewhere below my stomach, "Yes, Mother. I will find a way. I need to speak to Pelos now, is there a certain time you want this done?"

Vincent

Its been two days since the toxic residue from the monster blood was burned out of me by Valdís's blood. I haven't been able to face her since. I can't believe I was so stupid, so certain that no one would realize who I am. Man, the ego on this guy. I guess being out among the Outsiders allowed me to think entirely too highly of myself. Or maybe I was always an asshole.

I have been spending most of my time in the garden since then. My brothers seek me out occasionally. They tell me I should talk to her. I keep telling them I can't. I remember everything I did. And the scent of her now, it makes me hungry in other ways. I don't tell them I am afraid of me. Of my lack of control. What if I hurt her? What if I kill the woman we all waited centuries to find? How could I live with myself? How could they live with me? What if the me that isn't suffering from withdrawals is no more in control than the one that was?

It's just better if I leave her be until I am feeling stronger. I can sit here in the midst of the roses and breathe in their fragrance. Most of the time it keeps me from smelling her, but not today. Today, it's like she is here with me. I don't feel hungry for her so much today as I feel this bone deep longing to be in her company.

As if my longing has conjured her form, she walks into the rose garden and freezes when she sees me. "I didn't realize you were here. I'm so sorry, I'll just keep going through and be out of your way. I was just having a walk. I didn't mean to intrude on your solitude." She starts walking fast across the small space.

I realize she is truly here and not a dream conjured by

my mind. With a sigh, I give in to the longing, "Valdís, wait, stay. Please?"

She stops, mid-step, "Are you sure? Really? You don't have to spend time with me. I know your brothers are trying to talk you into having more to do with me, but I don't want to pressure you like that. I was just enjoying the gardens."

"Valdís, I asked you to stay. I want you to stay. I would very much like it if you would come sit on this bench with me. Will you please come sit with me?"

A half smile lifts one side of her gorgeous mouth and she says, "Promise not to bite?"

I bark out a laugh, "I promise that I will only ever again bite you with your express consent."

She smiles, "I was hoping it wasn't too soon for that joke." She walks over and seats herself on the bench, "How are you doing?"

I shrug, "I've been better. I feel really foolish right now, and shitty for how I treated you. I keep apologizing to my brothers for making them allow Eumeleia to remain now that I know how fucking horrible her scent is. I owe you for still being so adamant about saving my life, even though I would have taken yours."

She lifts a shoulder briefly, "You can really let go of those things. Addiction does terrible things and has people doing things they wouldn't normally do."

"Not good enough. I should have behaved better, no matter what."

She laughs at me, out loud and no attempt to hide it, "Vincent, do you honestly think you are the only person or vampire on the planet that should be able to avoid acting out because of an addiction? Sir, that's not how this works. Whether you choose to accept it or not, I'm not mad at you. Even if those actions are a part of you, we all have our flaws. My mom still kinda wants to murder you a little because you hurt me. That probably counts as a flaw, she could definitely be letting go of that already. I like cake a ridiculous amount and I am probably going to kill Eirene when I see her. Do I need to kill her? I don't think I do. I kind of want to though. I'm real damn mad about all she put me through. It's all things I could let go of but I don't think I will until all that is left of her is ash blowing in the wind."

I nod and inch my hand toward hers. I want to have my skin, even such a small bit, next to hers. To feel the heat of her on even a tiny piece of me. "I think that is more than understandable. She, Hekate, she took me to see you when you were young. I saw Eirene push you down a very steep hill in a way that was meant to seem accidental. As you tumbled down the hill, she said I couldn't interfere. Your father pushed Eirene into the wall, not believing for a moment that it had been an accident. The last thing he said to her before he started a more controlled descent, 'If she dies or suffers a permanent injury, you will too.' I was proud of Conrí in that moment. I asked Hekate if he would put her out then, she said no, he couldn't. Eirene was necessary. She would put into motion things that must happen for it all to culminate the way she hoped it would."

She looks away, "Thank you for telling me that. I always wandered why he didn't put her out. Divorce her. Lock her in the basement. Anything. When I asked, he never answered me, the subject was always changed. Hopefully Eirene isn't going to be needed after the next time I see her. I should probably ask about that."

Chuckling, I say, "hekate told me then that you might need to know things that your father couldn't bring himself to say out loud. You seem determined about killing Eirene, from what I have been told, that isn't exactly how you generally feel about killing."

She sighs and slumps a little, "You're right. It isn't. Eirene is a special case. Does that make you more certain that I am the evil in this world?"

Her voice is thick with emotion and I forget myself. My hands go to her shoulders of their own volition, turning her to face me. She turns her face away, keeping her head down, "Hey, look at me. Please?" She is still for long moments. When she does lift her head, I see the shine of unshed tears in her eyes. "I need you to know that I spoke out of turn and that I was projecting my own shit on you. It was easier than trying to figure out what the fuck was wrong with me, you know? You are not evil or even really evil adjacent."

She chuckles and the tears spills over, "Evil adjacent?"

Her hand lifts to swipe away the tears, I stop her by placing my hand over hers. When she sets it back down, I gently wipe away her tears. "I'm sorry I said that. I'm sorry I hurt you. I am really sorry that I tried to attack you. Twice. I hope you will forgive me and I want you to know that I am going to keep proving to you every day that I am not the person you first met." Is she breathing a little faster?

She inhales deeply, "I know that isn't who you are. We all could see you were struggling, none of us knew how to help. And that may be the root of it, we didn't know how to help and none of us thought to call in the one that did. This all could have been stopped so much sooner if I had called Hekate to ask."

She is breathing faster. Her heart rate is up. Oh! Oh. She's horny. Are my brothers nearby? I glance around, I don't see any of them. Is it me? Is it me she wants? She is looking at me with those big, beautiful eyes. Her lips open just a bit. I lean in, stopping just a bare inch from those full lips, "I want to kiss you."

She closes the distance, pressing her lips to mine, it feels like electricity running through my body. I can feel every cell in my body and they are all screaming for more contact with her. She wraps her arms around me, pressing her chest against mine as she deepens the kiss. Slowly, because I want to touch every inch of her, I move my hands, stroking her back. I need more contact, there is a fire raging in me that is going to leave me nothing but ash inside without her.

Breaking the kiss, I push her back, so I can get my hands on her waist. I lift her up, making her yelp as I set her on my lap. Her weight on my erection feels so damn good I moan and she rocks her hips, grinning down at me. Threading a hand into her hair I pull her down to kiss those full lips some more. Her hands trail fires across my chest and back as she explores. Her hips are rocking to her beat and I desperately want to be inside her. "I need you."

She breaks the kiss, leaning back a little to look at my face, "Want to see a trick I just learned?"

A trick? What? "Um, yes?"

Her grin grows wider as she lifts a hand and snaps her fingers. Everything is misty for a split second and then I feel her hot, wet lips pressed against my cock and I nearly explode. "Do you like my trick?"

Her breasts are bare in front of me and I can't form words. To show my appreciation I move a hand around to cup a breast and bring that big brownish pink nipple into my mouth. She sighs a little, and I suck hard. She moans and rocks her hips, coating my cock in her moisture. With a groan I release her nipple and move my hand back to her waist so I can lift her, freeing my cock to stand, pointing at her hot core. When I start to lower her, she puts her hands on my shoulders, "Let me," she whispers. A quick look to see she has her feet ready to support her weight and I move my hands to her breasts, bringing the other nipple to my mouth as she lowers herself. The first touch of her entrance to the head of my cock is bliss, I struggle not to come now. Then she starts making little circles with her hips, the head going a little further in with each circle. "Oh sweet fucking goddess, honey, it's been a very long time and you are going to end this before we get going, oh fuck me you feel so fucking good." She giggles, and then lowers herself onto me in one swift movement. "Oh fuck, oh! You are so damn hot and tight, oh yes. I am so sorry, I have to..."

Putting my hands on that big, juicy ass of hers to hold her up, I stand and drive myself a little deeper. She moans, and that is all the encouragement I need. Lifting her just a little, I start driving into her, hard and fast. Moments later, my world explodes as I empty myself in her with the best orgasm I can ever recall having.

When I am fully aware again, she is grinning at me. Then I hear Gage behind me, "About time you gave in to her. As you forgot she is supposed to come first, would you like me to take care of that?"

Laughing, I tell him, "I'm not finished, but if you want to join, I'm all right with that."

He says, "No, I wanted to make certain you weren't going to leave her wanting. I'll let you have this first time with her all to yourself. Valdís, I can't wait to see you later."

She smiles at him, "Me either Gage, me either."

I can see her love for him written on her face as I listen to his footsteps fade away. I want her to feel like that about me, oh Goddess, I need her to feel that way about me. "Aren't portals a thing you do?"

"Why, yes they are. Where would you like to go?"

"To a bed."

She tips her head to one side, "Mine or yours?"

"I would be honored to be invited to yours." Her breath catches and she looks for a moment like she wants to cry, "Did I say something wrong? We can go to mine."

She smiles as her hands move behind my head, "No, you didn't. I didn't think you would want to, that you, are you sure you want to be in the queens bed?"

"Very sure. Is your portal open?"

She giggles, "It's a bit filled at the moment. But I opened two. You can choose which room we go to. Left is mine, right is yours."

Turning, I head directly for the portal on the left. I know where I belong.

Sixteen

Eirene

Today is the day. We go to war in just a few short hours. The sun still sits below the horizon as I make ready. Nicholas is waiting in my bedroom. I would love to fuck the shyness out of him, but I really don't have time for it today. Perhaps he will be my treat when we come home, victorious.

Then I hear his voice, "We must talk before you leave this room. Tell him to wait outside."

Setting my brush down, I go to stand in the open door of my bathroom, "Nicholas, darling, please wait outside my bedroom. Our God would like to have a private word with me."

He salutes, in more ways than one as I am still in my underthings, blushes, and near races for the door. With a grin I turn and find my God standing in the bathroom behind me. "Is it ok for me to continue getting ready or would you prefer I not?"

He smiles, his eyes roaming my body, "Carry on. You'll remember my instruction well enough."

I love the feel of his eyes on me. Makes me feel all hard and soft in all the right places. Standing before the sink I start brushing my hair and coiling it into the up do I plan to wear today. Suddenly he is pressed against my back, one hand on my belly and the other pushing my panties down, moisture floods my core at the idea that I might get to have the cock of a god, my God, in me. He presses his hard length between my thighs, my panties around my thighs keeping me from spreading my legs. The hand on my belly moves to my back and presses me down toward the countertop, his other hand on my hip.

He says, "I'm going to fuck you Eirene. And when I finish, you are going to go take Atlantis with an army of monsters."

He pulls away and then drives into me. I cry out with the pain, but as he pulls out only to sink himself back into me, it begins to feel good. He removes his hand from my back and slaps my ass hard. I yelp and he does it again as he slams into me over and over. He puts his hand on the back of my neck, squeezing a little and pulling me up, his hand moving round to my throat as I rise. The hand that was on my hip moves to cup my mound, a finger hovering over my clit. He squeezes my throat lightly and whispers in my ear, "I'll transport your ships to a place out of sight of the coast of Atlantis, you'll stay there till night falls," he drives into me extra hard, causing me to cry out. I can't tell anymore if it is pain or pleasure. "When you get to shore, set the first boat of monsters loose. Let them destroy at will. As they start to move inland, always toward the castle, you will set the second boat free. There will be a key moment here," he punctuates the sentence by slamming into me, "and if you can knock Valdís out, you will win the day right then. If. You. Fail," slam, slam, slam, "there will be two more moments." He slams into me again and when his finger barely brushes my clit, a massive orgasm hits me. He never stops pounding me, "One will be when you arrive at the gates, if you shoot her when she is on her knees, you will end the war." Suddenly he buries himself deep inside me and I feel his seed shooting out of him. He withdraws, leaving me to lean on the sink and catch my breath. His seed, easing out of me feels strange. I hear things hitting the floor and I start to turn when he says, "Stay where you are till it is finished."

I turn my head to look at him, "Till what is finished?"

He smiles at me and I am, for the first time, frightened. "Why, the birth of our new monsters. Don't worry, it will be done in a few moments and in the next ten minutes you will have your fourth squad of monsters. These will be your personal monsters. Perhaps if you do well today, I will gift you with more."

I smile at him to cover my fear, "Oh, well, I suppose that is good. Is there anything else I should know about today?"

He smiles wider, as though he can tell how terrified I

am. "Only that it would not be good for you to fail. You can stand now, and adjust your clothing. I will be watching you on the battlefield." He disappears before my eyes. I don't know if I should cry, run away, or stay frozen. I am standing there, eyes still closed when I hear a voice, "It's ok, mother."

Oh God, what have you done to me? I open my eyes and I see many monsters standing around me and spilling out into the bedroom. One, I think possibly the one that spoke, puts a hand on my shoulder, "It was ill done of him to not warn you. But it will be all right."

Somehow, this is oddly comforting. I turn and look at him as I adjust my panties, "Do you have a name or is that something I need to give you?"

He shakes his head no, "We have names, he gave us those. Names and forms he gave us, but he couldn't give us life. He needed you to do that."

"He couldn't give you life? Then how did we, his people, come to be?"

He grins, a mouth full of teeth too sharp and too many, "He stole the original few from one of the other gods. He doesn't really want anyone talking about that though. We know because we lived inside him for so long. He took some people from other gods and made them his. And now, we are partly yours. Come, you must dress for the day Mother." He leads me from the bathroom and I think I must be in an alternate world, this can't be happening.

* * *

Eumeleia

Today is the day. Mother told me last night that I must wait until dinner time, they eat their evening meal as the sun goes down. That is when I am to create the distraction. I don't know what to do. Another tear slips down my face as I pull out the picture of Pelos that I keep with me always. "What do I do love? Should I do what she says, sentence us to a life of being bullied by her? Do I dare risk your life and mine by revealing all to the kings? Do I trust Valdís to rescue you when she has every reason to hate me?"

His picture is silent, but his voice rings in my ears anyway. I can hear all the times he told me to tell the kings everything. He wouldn't want this. Wouldn't want his homeland overrun for my mother's greed. Wouldn't want us both to live in fear the way we will if we live in my mother's homeland.

I know what I have to do. I kiss his picture, gently, making sure that I don't wet it with my tears. A fast trip into the bathroom has my face dried of any trace of tears. I can only hope it stays that way.

Leaving my bedroom I march to the dining room and throw open the door. The kings all grimace as I walk in and Valdís invites me to sit.

Opening my mouth, I try. I try to cause a scene but the words won't come out. My eyes burn as tears well up in them again, I blink fast to try and stop them, to no avail. Looking at the ceiling I say, "I'm sorry Pelos, I couldn't do it. I can't do what she wants." I look at them, they are all staring at me. "I'm sorry. I have to tell you the truth. I came here under false pretenses. My mother really did take Pelos, to force me to do her bidding. She is holding him hostage and when she finds out what I have done, she is going to kill him. So if you could just go ahead and kill me, that would be all right with me. I won't fight. I'll tell you everything, just kill me so that I can be with him." Swiping at my eyes, I can see now that the kings are pissed. "I was told to distract you all for two hours and to start about now. She will be on these shores not long after night falls. I'm so sorry."

The kings are all standing now, arguing about what to do with me. It is exactly the chaos she wanted and I worry that I may have accidentally done what she wanted.

Seventeen

Valdís

I knew it. My kings are not all surprised, I think the surprise is that she will be on our shores now. This is what we trained for. Standing, I say, "My Kings," rather forcefully and perhaps with a little magic behind it. Only to make sure they heard. They all look to me as I look to Eumeleia, "Will you let me rescue him now? We'll have to put you in a dungeon here, for our own safety. But I will fetch him for you, if you will let me. This is your chance, Eumie. Your last chance to be free of her, forever. Make your choice."

She sniffles, "Why would you do this for me? For us? Why? I don't understand?"

I shrug, "I never hated you Eumie. I didn't like the way you treated me, but the older I got the better I understood. I thought you were my sister, even when you were her stooge. You hated me for having boundaries and not protecting you from her. That wasn't my job. It wasn't my job to maintain your relationship with her by allowing you both to run over me. This is the person I am. You get to choose the person you are going to be in the future. Your time is running out, what is your decision?"

She is silent for a moment, staring down at the floor. Then she pulls a small frame from her pocket, and walks toward me. "Eumie, I can't do it quick from just a picture."

She flashes a wry, half smile, "You were right when you said I had been collecting pieces of him. That frame is made of his hair. I was afraid you would take him from me for spite."

I shake my head, "I wouldn't do that Eumie. That's something Eirene would do. Something Eirene did." I walk around her to a more open area of the dining room and cast the location spell as fast as I can. As soon as I have his location, I open the portal to him. He is in a cell and looks up in surprise when he sees it open. Eumie steps into view and he smiles so big, standing and walking across his cell to the portal. I lift the shield that we always include as he starts to step through. That's when I hear the shout, and a loud bang. Pelos seems almost pushed through the portal and I slam it closed as soon as he is fully out, before anything else can come through.

They have Pelos in a chair by the time I look at him, he was hit by something in the arm which is bleeding profusely. I open another portal and step through, knocking on Dagma's bedroom door. She is fully dressed when she answers and I tell her, "Come, we need you to heal Pelos."

She steps through the portal with me and dashes over to where he is bleeding still. Within moments he is healed and Malic has two guards taking them to the dungeon. They are grinning as they go, I don't think they care even a little where we put them, as long as they are together.

Malic

I look to my brothers as Valdís walks away. Eumeleia follows her and I am relieved we didn't have to tell her to do so. I dash over to the door and bellow out it for Epaphras, returning to the table I lean in to speak quietly with my brothers. "She's right, we have to send the two of them to the dungeon, Epaphras will ensure the guards take her phone away from her as well. And then we need to get out there and stop whatever she is bringing to our shores." I stop when I hear a shout and a shot, turning to see Pelos fall through the portal. Valdís closes it even as Gage has Pelos moved away to a chair. Valdís steps through a new portal and returns with Dagma. She has Pelos healed by the time Epaphras has arrived and fetched two guards before going off to start the preparations for the battles we will face tonight. Another portal opens and as witches pour into the room they quickly decide it is too small.

Chance says, "We have a ballroom, there is plenty of space for everyone there."

Valdís leads the way, a line of witches following her. It seems almost like they have practiced this, like a small army. Everyone has a job and they are moving seamlessly to carry out their tasks.

"We need to keep them here, where they will be safe." Gage and Chance laugh as they walk out of the room. Vincent walks over, puts a hand on my shoulder and says, "I don't think we are going to be able to keep the woman that stopped me in my tracks while I was trying to attack her in a blood craze. We may want to save our energies for things we can control." He squeezes my shoulder and then lets go, following Knox out of the room.

I shout in frustration, I know they are right. Then I walk my ass to the ballroom, grumbling about willful women that smell entirely too damn good.

Eighteen

Eirene

Four ships in a line. Each one stuffed with men and monsters. All of us watching for the sun to drop below the horizon and night to fall. We can't see it from here, but the island of Atlantis is less than an hour from us. For all that, all I can think about are the monsters surrounding me. Every one of the monsters on this ship slipped out of my pussy after my God fucked me. I don't know what to feel about this. I think I should be horrified. Scared. Anxious. And maybe I am a little of all of those.

But there is this other side of me that wants to do it again. All of it.

The sex with a God. The resulting monsters. The slight shame I felt after. I have never felt so alive as I do now and I am that much more determined to take this land and please my God. I need him to look upon me with favor, with lust.

And I have a new goal, I want to be a Goddess. I want

to be his Goddess. Together, we could rule this world. Tonight is the first step. He already wants me, he proved that this morning. I just need to convince him that he needs me at his side. Always.

One of my monsters touches my arm and I realize I have been in my thoughts and not paying attention to the setting sun. All the light is gone now and I tell him, "Go let our captain know to give the signal and head for Atlantis. Make sure he understands we need to be as silent as possible."

"Yes, it will be done, Mother."

Moments later the ships all start moving forward and my heart races with the excitement of a plan in motion.

Ingemar

There is something strange about this new set of monsters. They all watch her like she is their everything. Her every breath a joy for them and it is real fucking creepy. We've been sitting here in the ocean watching the damned sun go down for what seems like days, but I think it was only an hour or so. Eirene has been in a trance staring out over the ocean for the last little bit as the sun went down. One of her creepy monsters just alerted her to the sun having set. The ship lights up and begins to push through the darkness. It isn't long before I see other lights in the distance. My homeland. I look around at the monsters surrounding me and a small pang of sorrow for the land

and my people hits me, but I push it aside. Pelos and I will be among the only Atlanteans left after tonight. There is no saving this place. But we may be able to keep ourselves alive and that is all I really care for anyway. I never cared for the land itself and the people certainly were only ever a means to an end.

Looking at her, I ask, "Will we be following the monsters in?"

She nods, "We are. We will follow in their wake, the monsters with us will take care of any stragglers that the first three waves missed. There will be no survivors when we have finished here. My God has waited a long time for the right moment to do this and I fully intend to make sure that all goes according to plan. Does this bother you? Do you need to be held here on the ship?"

My heart nearly stops at the idea that she may not trust me, I need her to trust me. A flash of the last time I saw Kleitos passes through my mind and I hurry to reassure her, "No, no. It bothers me not at all. I am eager to see the end of this place."

She smiles, "Good. I will have a special job for you. Is your aim still as good as it once was?"

"Yes, why?"

"You'll see. We are nearly there now, your questions will have to wait."

What does she want me to do?

Nineteen

Valdís

In the ballroom my witches start opening the small, shielded portals to various places on our coastline just like we practiced. It seems almost immediately one of them finds the place on the coast where they are arriving. The woman, Isa, calls me over, "Valdís, you have to see this." I go to where she is and she says, "These, they, they are't human." Her eyes are wide and showing a lot of the whites, I turn to call Dagma and she is behind me.

"Have you got her?" She nods and I leave Isa to her gentle care as I step around her to have a look through the portal. What I see is like nothing I could have imagined. They are people shaped. But that is where the similarity ends. They are eating our people. So many teeth. Why are there so many teeth in a human size head? Are some of them scaled? Holy fuck. I see why Isa is not ok. Turning to Isa I say, "We need to make it bigger so everyone can see." I put a hand on her shoulder and feed her more energy. She turns from my mom and focuses on the portal. Hands moving through the air she turns it into a much larger circle. I am entirely grateful for the shield that protects us from projectiles even as it keeps us from being seen.

By the time she is done the other portals are closed and my kings are over here to see what we have seen. Their faces are grim as they look. We can see the ships at the shoreline, their fronts opened to the beach and monsters pouring out. I watch as Eirene walks off a ship, Ingemar next to her.

I hate her fucking smile. I hate that she is doing this to my family. Family. That's what all these people are, they are the family I never really had. My father tried, but it's hard to be a loving father while you are stuck in a situation that will eventually lead to your death. These people that I collected around me, they are my family. Quorin and Lommán in the corner whispering with the other council members. Dagma and the two K's comforting witches that are panicking a little seeing the monsters rampaging through our lands. All of the witches that we have rescued. Bettina, the first witch we found, who kept my mother protected while she murdered men left and right to come save me. My kings, preparing themselves for what they think will be their last battle in the hope that their sacrifice will save us.

She can't have them. Eirene took my father from me, she won't take another damn person from me. No more of my family will fall to her, no matter what we have to do. I catch Quorin's eye and raise my brows, she nods and goes back to her part of the plan. I realize my kings are preparing to leave now and I shout, "No! Wait! You can't go yet!"

Knox comes to hug me and then with his hands on my arms he says, "Valdís, this is what we were made for, why we have lived so long. We have to go out there. It's our job."

The rest of them nod in agreement behind him. I shake my head no, "If you go now, you'll be swarmed in minutes and killed, your deaths will be for nothing. Let us help you! We can shield you and the guards. We'll make it hella hard for them to kill any of you. And, we are setting guards into the towns to evacuate people to the castle. Or just out of the path to the castle if they refuse to come here. Even now," I point to a group of women in another corner, "they are working on a shield to slow them. It won't stop them but it will give our people time to get away. Plus, it might help convince them we are a lot weaker than they guessed."

Knox looks at the others and then turns back to me, "All right, but we need to get out there as soon as possible."

"Excellent." The ladies in the corner working on the shield nod at me and I tell Isa, "Move your portal, the shield is going up." She is fast and gets it to the next spot in time for us to see the first monsters run into the shield face first, full speed. On the other side of the ballroom, Epaphras is working with the group of witches assigned to porting guards out to evacuate. Yet another group of witches is shielding those guards before they go through the portals.

Quorin catches my eye as she leaves the ballroom, one quick nod and she is gone.

Chance

Malic, Knox, and Vincent are pacing. They are angry at the wait, chomping at the bit to get covered in blood. Gage is standing next to me, arms folded across his chest. I look over at him, "She's fucking magnificent, isn't she?"

He nods, "I think our brothers didn't notice all the training the witches were doing. And certainly none of the plotting. I confess I don't know all they have planned, but I have faith in our Valdís. If we make it through this, she'll be why."

"I think she is opening our door. Ready to go cleave some skulls?"

He pulls his sword from its sheath in answer. I pull mine and we all wait a few moments more while the witches shield us and then Valdís says, "You come back alive or I'll hunt you down and bring you back dammit."

We each give her a quick kiss as we pass her to go through the portal, dozens of guards pouring through along with us.

* * *

Valdís

My kings never even suspected when I told them to come back alive that they would not be the only ones to go through that portal. Once all the guards going with them are through, Bettina, Dagma, the two K's, and I also step through the portal. The two K's are immediately growing things, vines and trees wreaking havoc among the monsters. Bettina shields us, this shield seeming slightly opaque. Dagma is dropping monsters left, right, and center. My job is shooting them with fire and ice. I am throwing lances that grow and sharpen further as they fly. I can't even see the kings any more. Or the guards. I have to believe they are just out of sight because the thought that one of them might be... not ok causes a feeling to rise that I think is going to be really bad for everyone if I don't keep it tamped down. It feels like a hot, sharp edge between panic and rage trying to come up razor sharp and ready to destroy it all.

The monsters have finally noticed us and they are swarming us, I put a hand on Bettina. Feeding her energy as I tell her, "Don't you let that shield fail! No matter what!"

Her eyes are wide and her lips pressed together as she nods. The bodies are getting thrown out of the way as fast as we kill them. There's so many! Dagma screams, "They are digging under! Extend the shield! Make it a sphere! Hurry!"

Bettina does it and we smell burnt flesh from the monsters that were cut by the shield in the process. Burnt flesh, there's an idea. I envelope the shield in flames in a pulse and the shrieks of pain from those damn monsters are pretty fucking satisfying. Even if it does really intensify that stench.

Twenty

❧

Malic

Why the fuck are they trying to avoid me now? Swinging my sword I catch one as he tries to run past. I look back to see what the fuck they are running to, are my brothers in need of help? Are they getting swarmed? And then I see a bubble that keeps pulsing with fire and my heart stops. A roar explodes from my throat as I run for the flimsy fucking bubble protecting our queen.

They are swarming her and she keeps covering the shield in flames to back them off. My sword is sending parts of these monsters flying. It's still multiple monsters between their shield and me. I realize my brothers are fighting next to me, we are cutting these fuckers down all over the place but it doesn't seem to be helping.

We finally make it to the shield and we form a second barrier around them, our swords cutting through everything coming at us, a pile of corpses growing to create another barrier. Another wave of monsters comes at us, running past guards still fighting. There are so many, how are we going to stop them all? Even we have limits to what we can do.

They reach us and it's all I can do to keep up, even as I see the lances of ice and fire fly out, slicing through monsters. We just have to keep her safe, if we can do that, I won't mind dying. Unless maybe it's being bit by one of these fuckers. That many teeth is just fucking creepy.

Eirene

None of them have any idea that I am watching. Between them and the little bitches in the bubble, they've nearly cut through the entire first ship of monsters. I just need to wait for them to get into position, then I can release the next set.

I put the binoculars up to my eyes just in time to see them position themselves with their backs to the bubble, that's what I was waiting for. Turning toward the beach I flash a light in that direction twice. The first batch from the second ship go directly for the kings. Once they are past I turn to the beach again and flash my light three times, watching as the rest of the monsters from the second ship runs past everyone toward the castle.

"Come, we need to get closer. The moment is nearly upon us. We need to be within dart range."

* * *

Quorin

The front door to the castle has been thrown open and we have an assembly line getting people from here to the protected space under the castle. People are arriving every which way, on foot, hanging off vehicles, and some are daring the portals we have set up. When Valdís first started talking about this plan, I thought her cheese must've slipped off her cracker. I had no idea there was really a whole giant bunker under the castle created just to keep our people safe. The kings didn't even seem to like us before all this started, why would they have created that? But here we are. The space is real and it may be the only thing that allows any of our people to survive this night.

Not everyone is ok with the portals, no matter how fast it is to simply step through from one place to another. The guards that are going to stay with our people have been instructed to take them via the secret passages to the other castles if we should fail. Fuck I hope this works. The guards at the gates run out and grab the last of our people as we hear the first howls of the monsters. The sound sends chills through my body. My Lommán comes running through the gates carrying an old couple like sacks of grain and shouting, "Close the gates! Close the gates!"

I start working on the shield that has to hold the monsters back while we get everyone inside. We weren't planning for monsters. I can only hope it will hold long enough. More than half our witches are out setting shields for the other castles. We hope it doesn't come to that but, if we fall, it will buy our people some time to get in the boats and get away. The gates slam shut for the first time in a very long time even as monsters start hitting my shield. I feed more power into it even as I start to withdraw to the castle. Our people are mostly inside when the portals start appearing. Witches step through and I ask, "Is it done? Were there any problems?"

One of them, Milla, says, "The castles were empty, it was just a matter of making sure that no one could get in that didn't belong. We put some special surprises in the tunnels, just in case."

"Good! Let's get in the castle before they break through my shield."

We all retreat into the castle, the guards slamming the doors shut as soon as we clear them. They throw the bar and I release the shield at the gates, letting it seem like they broke through. Taking the hand of Milla on one side and Isa on the other as they hold hands with other witches and we form a quick circle to set a shield on the doors. It won't be drawing on our power continually, but its power is finite and it will fail. We can only hope that Valdís makes it back before then.

The sound of the metal screeching as the gates give way before the flood of monsters is terrifying. Luckily, we have finished setting the shield. It will hold them back from the doors, for a time.

Lommán makes his way to me, taking me in his arms. I find the same solace there I always do and I wrap my arms around him, sinking into his embrace even as I hope to Hekate that it isn't for the last time. He releases me and says, "I'll be right here beside you, it's you and me, always."

Tears spring to my eyes as I remember the last time he said that, we both nearly died. Would have died if his mom hadn't been so determined to save us. With as much of a smile as I can muster I say, "Hopefully we'll both do better at protecting ourselves than last time."

He smiles ruefully, "I think we might do a little better. We have a few more tricks up our sleeves than we had then."

The monsters start howling at the doors, clawing at the shield to get through. All we can do is face the doors and wait, listening while they work to rip away the shield. The doors won't last long once the shield fails. Come on Valdís, where are you? We all feel it when the shield falls. The doors shake in their frame when the monsters make it to them. "All right, get in place everyone. We knew it might come to this. Let's find out how much time we can buy our people."

Even as everyone moves, I feel the portal open behind me and I could cry with the relief of it.

Twenty-One

Valdís

The field is cleared. Holy fuck, I wasn't sure it would ever happen. Bettina drops the shield and I take my hand from her shoulder. Before Dagma can run off to heal everyone I grab her arm and hold my other hand out to her. She puts her hand in mine with a grin and I make sure that her well of power is full. I know she is about to heal everyone she can and I'll need to do this again. She leans in and kisses my cheek, "You are a good daughter. Come, let's move fast, those at the castle are going to need us there now. That castle wasn't built with monsters in mind."

I laugh as I release her, "Seems like a design flaw to me, we should talk to the builders." The two K's are looking tired as I refill their power. "Are you ok? Do you need healing?"

Kalina laughs, "We need youth and vigor. We are old and it is past our bedtime."

Katerine nods, "She is right. We are old. Were all this excitement not happening, we would have been in bed with the setting of the sun. Or having a late dinner with you. Our lives aren't usually nearly so exciting as all this."

I finish topping them off and tell them, "Ok, I'm still going to have Dagma check you over before we go."

They nod and I turn away to find Dagma. Of course I can't see her for the kings crowded around me. Malic is the one that says, "What are you doing?"

"Going to find Dagma and refill her power. No one else seems to have the unending well I have."

When I would have stepped around him he grabs me by the arms and lifts me off the ground to set me back in front of him, "That isn't what I meant and you know it. What are you doing on the battle field? You weren't supposed to be here."

Oh Malic, if you only knew how violent I feel about your attitude right now. "Malic, I need you and the rest of you kings to listen real close and heed my words. One of us had plans for this battle that didn't start and end with you five running out to kill the monsters with your swords. You can help me or I will put you out of my way. We could use your help at the castle in a few, that's where the other monsters ran when they bypassed us. You are slowing me down. Now, what will it be? Portals out or work with me?"

Malic runs a hand down his face, smearing the blood all over it. Eventually growling out, "Fine. We'll do it your way. But I don't like you being in danger."

Laughing, I tell him, "I don't like you all being in danger either. Now move."

He steps to the side and I run to find Dagma. Her power was almost gone, but she has healed all the fatigue and small injuries. The shields put on the guards and my kings are really doing the trick, keeping them from being badly injured. We go back to where we came in and I open the portal to the castle. We send the guards through first. It seems like so many more than when I first came to the castle. Some of them look so young, I hate this for them. That they should be spending this time fighting a war that began before they were born. Once they are through, the two K's make their way through, followed by Dagma and Bettina. My kings go next, except for Gage, who insists on walking me through. When something hits me as I walk through, I'm really glad he did. He shouts with rage and fear as he scoops me up and takes me the rest of the way through. I wave a hand at the portal to close it behind us. I feel so woozy, what did they do to me? I hear Gage calling for Dagma, but it sounds like I'm under water. Dagma pulls something out of my arm and starts cursing even as she heals me. The woozy, underwater feeling recedes as she does and I realize, listening to her string of curses, she is pissed because they tried to drug me again. The dart in her hand is filled with that same drug they used before.

She says, "Those fuckers tried to knock you out. They are still trying to take you, Valdís."

"Well fuck that. I don't wanna go. And their drugs suck."

The doors fail completely and I realize the noise I have been hearing in the background was monsters clawing and beating at the doors. As the doors fall monsters pour through, running up the door to jump down into the castle even before the doors hit the ground. My kings stand ready before us, still coated in the blood of monsters. I cast a worried look at Vincent, but he is standing strong.

The doors crash to the floor and there are monsters everywhere. It's hard to aim with the constant movement of everyone. I do the best I can, freezing body parts instead of setting things on fire, until one of the monsters tries jumping up onto the backs of everyone and running toward us. Chance snatches the first to the floor and Vincent skewers the second one.

But that is when I realize once they are up in the air, I don't have to worry I am going to hit any of my people. With a grin I start firing at everything that jumps up above the crowd, bunches of needles of ice, spreading as they fly through the air. The blood spraying on me from the fighting in front of me is not great, but not like they can do anything about that. The two K's are flagging, but they have multiple monsters dying slowly in plant cocoons and I think maybe some have been fed to carnivorous plants that suddenly have one or two unusually large blooms. Quorin is keeping the three fighters before her protected as best she can. Dagma is dropping monsters as fast as she can. They are all looking fatigued, but if I go to refill them, I leave a hole.

Bettina seems to be blunting claws and teeth by

shielding them. I watch one of the monsters surprise as she accidentally fills his open mouth with a shield but then my attention is drawn away by a group of monsters leaping to the top of the crowd and running at us. Shots are fired from behind me even as I start firing. I remember all the women behind me and I motion for a few of them to take my place. When they are in place and firing at the monsters I run the line of witches, refilling wells of power as I go.

Eirene

"Dammit! She made it through the portal! Fuck!" I pace a little bit, "It's fine. This is fine. He said there are a couple opportunities for this and now she is going to be mostly, if not completely, incapacitated. There were enough drugs in that dart to knock out a, a monster."

I turn and shine the light toward the boats once more and the next group of monsters begins to make their way to the castle. This has to work. These stupid kings and my idiot stepdaughter cannot ruin my chance to become a goddess. I will not allow it to happen. I watch as they swarm past. The destruction left in their wake seems like a waste of energy but, they seem to be unable to help themselves. I wonder who the woman was that was part of making them? Does that have anything to do with it? Perhaps they are... less refined because of who their mother is, or was. Once they are past us, I flash the light at the boats once more.

My monsters, my sons, come running from the boat and directly to me, joining with the few that I allowed to stay with me as guards. Moving so that I can face the people and monsters with me, I raise my hands to get everyone's attention, "Gentlemen, it is time. We go now to finish the taking of this land by killing the kings and claiming the key. Do not, under any circumstances, allow that key to die. Our God wants her alive and it is our job to make certain that he gets what he wants. Or the next thing he will want is our heads. Do not fail me and you won't fail him. Let's go."

One of my sons scoops me up while the others grab up the rest of my entourage, the ones that can't keep up anyway.

Twenty-Two

Vincent

The number of monsters has dwindled and looking for the next one I see a guard kill the last of them. It looks like most of the guard survived. Fuck, I haven't been this tired since we fought the first monster before we became what we are now. I look over at my brothers, they are covered in blood the same as I am and just as tired. Chance has sat himself down on a convenient pile of bodies. Where is she? I look around the room and I find her moving through the witches, putting her hands on them, refilling them. Encouraging them.

We don't fucking deserve her.

I hear the howls and I look at my brothers, we all share the same resigned look. This is the end. We, none of us, has enough left to fight another battle of this magnitude. This is the end of Atlantis. Even still we, and the guards that are left, kick the bodies out of the way and plant ourselves as they come boiling through the gate. Then Valdís steps through us like she is walking out to greet them. I start to reach for her but she is suddenly covered in flames. I realize what is about to happen and I yell, "Take cover!"

My brothers and I stand side by side behind her, our bodies acting as a wall for anyone without the time to hide. The fire covering her becomes an inferno as the monsters run across the courtyard, and then the air is an oven as the fire shoots out from her body. Most of the fire and heat shoots out the opening that had doors not long ago, the smell of the monsters flesh as it burns is sickening and I hear various people retching.

The heat and flames are painful from where we are, but nothing our bodies can't cope with. It just goes on and on. I start to wonder if she even can turn it off or will she burn till there is nothing left of herself when it cuts off. For brief seconds I can't see, but I hear her collapse to the ground. I head for her even before my eyesight has fully returned. She is pushing herself onto her knees as we get to her. The first thing she says is, "Did I get them all?"

Eirene

The castle looks like it was on fire. I can smell charred flesh everywhere. It has an odd smell and I feel a pang of unease as my monster sets me down inside the courtyard. It looks scorched and there are piles of ash everywhere.

My monsters and I walk to the castle, I see the kings

surrounding Valdís as she struggles to get to her feet from the floor. "Valdís, so good to see you again. Be a dear and give yourself up to one of my monsters, it will all go much easier for you if you come willingly. As for you kings, well, your time is over. The ruling of this country is not yours any longer, if you will move away from our key, my monsters will be happy to help you into whatever afterlife there is for creatures such as you that feed off the life force of others to survive."

The vampire kings put themselves in front of her like they think they will be able to protect her, I laugh at their pitiful attempts. Any fool can see they have nothing left. I pull out my gun and start to turn to my monsters when suddenly Dagma is before me, her face a mask of rage. "You will never touch my child again, bitch!"

Before I can answer, my chest is tight. I can't breathe, and the world goes dark.

Ingemar

She died, oh fuck. What do I do now? The monsters are frozen, staring at her like they are waiting for something. I look back at Eirene and she twitches, then pushes herself up off the ground, laughing. Her voice is strange as she says, "Fools. You opened the gateway for me to stand on this soil again. Everything you have done will matter naught, this land is mine now."

The laughter that bubbles up out of her is terrifying

and I feel a warm liquid running down my leg as I recognize where I have heard that voice before. It was in her office. Oh fuck me, it's her God. Her God has possessed her. What the fuck kind of God is this that he needs to possess someone to stand here on this land?

I realize now, entirely too late, that Pelos was right. I chose wrong.

Valdís

I am still on my knees trying to figure out what to do when I hear Hekate's voice. "You broke the rules Divinus. Do you know what happens when you break the rules? Did you decide these consequences were worth it? I think perhaps you did not."

She stops beside me, extending a hand to me that I take with gratitude. "I'm so damn glad you are here."

She smiles, "So am I."

The God in Eirene's body is blustering, "I broke no rules! You are just mad that you lost! This land is mine and that key," he/Eirene points directly at me, "is mine! I've won it and you can't handle that!"

Hekate smiles and says, "Mother, it's time for you to come out now."

Another woman steps out of the wall behind Divinus/Eirene and walks over to stand next to us. Divinus/Eirene pales as they watch her, "What is she going to do? She is nothing to me! She's no part of the ruling body. She has no power over me!"

Hekate laughs, "You are correct, my mother is not part of the ruling body. But my daughter is. Darling, would you care to share the judgement and sentence the ruling body came to?"

A voice echoes through the building, "Divinus, you are found guilty of possessing a body in the manner of a demon, of creating monsters without the consent or knowledge of the woman used to do so, of stealing the power of other deities, attempting to steal power from yet more deities in order to become a supreme being, and wanton destruction of a land not your own. For these crimes and more, you are sentenced to live out eternity in that body, sharing it with its original owner who matches you in many ways. Both of you will be completely stripped of power. We have created a small dimension where you and your monsters will spend your eternity."

Divinus/Eirene screams and turns to run, but falls as their feet are tangled in vines. I look back at the two K's and they grin at me. Turning back to face the proceedings I watch as the monsters disappear one at a time while Divinus/Eirene pulls frantically at the vines. All of their efforts manage nothing as they disappear.

The voice continues on, "You that came to this land at their bidding, you must make a choice. Will you go home or stay and become Atlanteans for the rest of your natural lives?"

One of them speaks up, "Will we be held accountable for their crimes if we stay?"

"No."

He looks around at his people, they all nod and he says, "If it is all the same, we would prefer to stay. If we go back, nothing good will happen to us."

"Very well," we watch as something ripples over them, "you are Atlanteans, body and soul now. Your goddess is Hekate, should you choose to worship her. Ingemar, you are subject to the governing body of this land. You made your choices over and over of your own free will and based on greed and envy." He slumps to the ground, as though unconscious. "Mother, I wish you and Grandmother well as I have joined the ruling body permanently. I will not be allowed to publicly or privately acknowledge our relationship again. Please know that you are loved and you may always call on us for aid."

I see a tear slip down Hekate's cheek, "I knew you were destined for great things. Be well and know that I love you and will always. Goodbye, my little love."

It is at that point that Ingemar jumps up and tries to run away. Two of the men originally from the land of the Outsiders grab him and hold him in place while some of our guards walk over to collect him. Hekate turns to me and her mother walks over to stand next to her. The likeness between them is amazing. Hekate looks at her mother who nods and then back to me, "We have an offer for you." She pauses for a moment, looking down. "I wasn't entirely concerned with what being my key would do to you or how it might change you when I sent it forward in time. All I knew was that you were the best place to hide the key. I did not anticipate that it would change you. That you would begin to transition into a goddess in your own right as you used the power within you. Or that it was even possible for that to happen."

"A what? What does this mean?"

She lifts a shoulder briefly, "Well, that depends on you. We can take the key from you. You would not be injured in any way. You would still have all your power. Your life would be unnaturally extended. We could connect that of your kings to yours, so that they would live as long as you. You would essentially be just a witch after a few hundred years or so, though still the most powerful there ever was or will be."

Her mother takes over then, "Or, the key could remain where it is. Over time you would develop further into the role of Goddess, whether you intended to or not. You would be like a sister to Hekate, and another Goddess to this land. You would not be allowed to rule as queen ever and your kings would have to either choose to stay with you or stay as kings, they could not do both."

Gage interrupts her then, "We go with her."

She raises a brow at him, "Just like that, without even knowing what she will choose?"

Vincent answers, "Yes. Just like that. We don't deserve her and we will follow where she leads in the hope that one day we might be deserving of her." Each of my kings nods their agreement and I think I might cry. They are worth ten of me and they have no idea.

She continues on, "You would also need to spend time outside this realm on a regular basis. They would be allowed to move through realms with you."

"I wouldn't be allowed to keep my mother with me forever, would I?"

"No, but you would be allowed to stay until her passing, even as extended as she has ensured it will be." She looks directly at Dagma when she says that and I turn to look at her too. She is blushing, smiling as she shrugs. I look back to Hekate's mother, "We would not force you to leave during her lifetime. Cruelty, though the evidence would seem otherwise, is not in our nature. However, you have time to make your decision. I am going home now. I have had enough of the air here, it is odd after being in my home so long and I really only needed to play witness anyway. I just couldn't resist meddling. She was on the fence because she didn't want to push you one way or the other. I have no such compunction. I'll see you soon dear."

With that last pronouncement as she looked me in the eye, she disappears. I look at Hekate, "Is all that true?"

She sighs, "Yes. She was worried I wouldn't tell you all of it because I don't want to sway you unfairly."

I nod, "I see. And what would you prefer I do?"

"Become one of us. In holding the key for so long, you have become connected to me and I, I would like it to remain so. The older we get the less connection we have and the connections are what keep us more... more humane."

"May I have time to think about this? I know your mother said I have time, but are you ok with it if I take some time to think about this?"

"You may. You may take as long as you like. You have only to call me when you have made your decision." I nod and she disappears before my eyes like her mother did.

Twenty-Three

Valdís

"I think today might just be the most beautiful day ever."

Knox laughs, "You've said that every day, rain or shine, since Divinus and Eirene were taken away to their dimension."

"That's because each one is the most beautiful day ever so far. And today is better than most because today is the wedding!" They smile at me, my kings, fully in support of my joy over this wedding. I stand from the table we have had our breakfast at, "I need to go join everyone else in getting ready, I'll see you there. I just wanted to have breakfast with you before we were separated for hours."

Leaning down I give Knox a kiss and then turning to the other side, Chance gets his. By the time I have finished, Gage, Malic, and Vincent are behind me, waiting for theirs.

I take off at a run after, I can't wait to put on my dress! This is going to be the best wedding ever.

We have taken over one of the sitting rooms for all the women to get ready in and there are shrieks when I open the door. "Close the door! Someone will see!"

Inside I see the two K's, for all the world looking like little old fairies. They even put on wings today, calling themselves garden fairies. I ask them, "Did you get the gardens ready?"

Kalina says, "The gardens are gorgeous, now get your dress on! Your breakfast with the kings cost you a lot of time. Have you called her yet?"

I work at getting my clothes off as I reply, "Well, no. But I talked to her yesterday. She said she would be here the instant I call her."

They hand me my dress and while I put it on they tell me, "Good. We don't want any slip ups today. We worked entirely too hard on making sure that garden would be filled to bursting with flowers today."

I laugh, "You would think it is your wedding the way you two act!"

Katerine smiles, "Oh honey, this one is so much more important than either of our weddings were. Get your shoes on. One of the ladies will get your makeup done. Hurry up now, it's going to take too long as it is!"

Shoving shoes on my feet I take a seat next to Dagma who is getting her makeup done right now. She winks at me and I grin before the woman doing my makeup says, "Stop that, I need you still for this."

While the time passes quickly for us, chatting and excited as we are, it is hours later when the entire wedding party is ready. Most of the women leave the room to go take their seats out in the garden. The rest of us follow at a more sedate pace, and we stop just before we would round the corner and come into the view of everyone. The two K's were not exaggerating about their work on the flowers. They are everywhere and the very air is saturated with their scents. I call Hekate and she appears at the end of the aisle with the thunderclap she promised would happen. Seconds later the music starts up and the procession down the aisle begins. First is the two K's, holding hands and skipping down the aisle in their fairy finery as they make it rain flower petals from the wands they created this morning. Then Dagma makes her journey up the aisle, followed by Bettina. Finally it is my turn and I walk up the aisle, my dress matching Dagma and Bettina's exactly. Beautiful, jewel toned red dresses, knee length with fluffy tulle skirts. Once I have taken my place next to them, the wedding march begins and we all turn to watch Quorin walk down the aisle. Her dress is all gold and black, form fitting with a long train trailing out behind her. She declined a veil and is wearing her hair in an updo with a few curls draping artfully. But the most beautiful thing is the smile on her face and the love in her eyes as she looks at my brother Lommán waiting for her at the end of the aisle.

The two of them are glowing as Hekate performs the ceremony. When she finishes and they kiss, we all cheer like mad, I think the entire kingdom may be able to hear us.

Later, after the reception and the happy couple leaving for the southern-most castle for a week or three of honeymoon, I am sitting in the garden with my lovers. We are in the rose garden, sitting in one of the grassy areas. Vincent looks over at me, "What about you? Are you happy? Do you need a wedding or something?"

Laughing, I tell him, "No. I don't need a wedding. That has never been my dream. But Quorin, she deserved to have the most beautiful wedding of her dreams that was possible and, I think she got that. I know she married the love of her life, and she is certainly the love and light in Lommán's life. It makes my heart sing to see the two of them so happy. Speaking of happy, did you see Eumeleia and Pelos at the wedding? Doesn't she just glow now that she is carrying Pelos's child? She has everything she ever wanted with him. And with their parents gone."

Gage nods, "Have you made your choice?"

"I think I have. I suppose you want to know what it is?"

Malic growls, "Yes, little trouble, we would like to know. You've kept us all in suspense for weeks now."

"I suppose I have. Well, I— are you sure you don't want to have some kind of say in this?"

Knox glares at me, "Valdís. Get on with it."

"Very well. I chose to be a Goddess. I decided to keep the key within me and become a Goddess."

Hekate appears, sitting in the grass next to me, "Its about time you shared your decision. Welcome to the fold, sister." She leans over and hugs me tightly, I throw my arms around her, still amazed that I can do this now.

She releases me and says, "I am glad you chose this. And, now that you have chosen. I didn't want to tell you this before because I feel it would have unfairly biased you this way. But, you should know that you can populate your dimension with whomever you like and that time moves differently, sometimes not at all, in other dimensions. Meaning that lives are greatly extended. You, of course, must have their consent to take them there with you, but, whoever you choose that agrees to it... well, I think you get my drift. Have a lovely night!"

She disappears while my jaw is still dropped. "I would swear she said I couldn't take anyone with me..."

Chance says, "She did. Looks like she really wanted to keep from swaying your decision. We all know how much your mother and grandmothers mean to you. She was likely concerned that you would take on being a goddess simply to keep them alive and with you."

"I would. I would absolutely have immediately take it on without another thought just for the possibility that I would get to keep them. I suppose at some point I'll have to figure out how to get there, but that's a problem for another day. For now, would you men like to go fool around with a goddess?"

Epilogue

Valdís

My mother and the two K's were thrilled when I told them that they could go to my dimension with us. I was more than a little shocked when they asked if they could bring their boyfriends with them. Apparently a couple of the guards liked being groped and sought them out after they apologized. In all the times that I dreamt of maybe having a grandmother or two, that they would suddenly take up with men much less than half their age never made it into my dreams.

Dagma, I asked her if their was anyone she was interested in, or if she would like to come back periodically to try and find someone. She said she had never really had any interest in anyone romantically, it just wasn't her thing. That was part of why she was willing to have a child in a way that guaranteed she didn't have to have sex with anyone.

We all stayed at the castle for long enough to see Quorin and Lommán when they came back from their honeymoon, sun-kissed and happy. They, and the rest of the council, were sad to see us go but eager to start making sweeping changes to the way things had been done.

Hekate came back many times while we were there to teach me how to slip between dimensions and more importantly, how to take other people with me. She agreed that it is time for our people to come out of hiding and the council is now in contact with the rest of the world. With one exception. The land of the Outsiders is in turmoil currently and all the deities are going to meet soon to decide what to do with the people of that land. They are all descended from peoples that were kidnapped, lost to their families and deities. They were ruled harshly by Divinus and now that their leadership is all gone, they are at a loss.

One of the other Goddesses sent some of her people to stop the monsters rampaging. She told Hekate and I that when they felt him disappear, the monsters that weren't sent with him went a little rogue and started killing everyone. I confess, I am not entirely sad that pretty much all the heads of his religion were being held in the castle by the monsters and were the first ones to die.

But the people of that land are a problem for another time. Right now, it is finally time to take my little family to my dimension. Hekate and her mother created it for me and it is a good place. I have visited it a lot recently for practice but I never took anyone with me to it. When I practiced taking people with me, we went to Hekate's dimension. I wanted to keep mine a surprise.

But today is the day that we all go to my dimension. The two K's have requested that I check into whether or not I could possibly make their bodies feel a little younger in my dimension. I am mildly horrified and very glad that I created a little house for the two of them and their guards to have all the privacy I could possibly need for them to have.

The Witches Council have all gathered to say goodbye. I will not cry, dammit. Quorin steps forward, taking my hands, "You will come back to visit us, won't you?"

"Of course! And, Hekate taught me how to hear my name if it is called. You can call on me, if you need me or just maybe need a visit from your sister in law."

She smiles, her eyes bright with tears, "Living in that house working for your father and Eirene, I could not have imagined anything like this. Hearing you call me sister in law, it just reminds me that all my dreams have come true. And then some. Who would have guessed that I would be part of the ruling council for our land and be part of the reason why we are in contact with the rest of the world? Oh Valdís, we couldn't have done this without you. Are you quite sure you have to go?"

I pull her in for a hug, my own tears falling, "I am not gone forever. You and everyone here, you are my family. I couldn't have made it to here without you all. You all are my touchstone, my heart. I meant it when I said you can call on me for anything. And even if you don't, I am coming back to see you. Lommán has already told me about your plans to adopt. I cannot wait to meet your children. You and he are going to be the best parents ever."

It takes us both a little time to stop sobbing on each other, but eventually we do and I move on to finish saying my goodbyes. Everyone leaves us and we walk through the castle one more time to the queen's suite. Epaphras walks with us, telling us about how the transfer of the spy network Malic had setup is going. He hugs each of us and presses a kiss to my forehead, saying, "If I had been so blessed as to have a daughter, I would have considered myself the luckiest man alive if she were anything like you. Come back and see me, I will miss you."

The tears I thought were done came back in full right then, leaving my voice watery as I tell him "Thank you, I will see you soon."

He nods and hurries out of the room, locking the door behind him as he closes it. I look around at my little family, and we form our own little circle, holding hands. Once we are all connected, I call the power and take us home.

Rhiannon writes steamy paranormal romance. She is an avid reader of many authors in a variety of genre though she tends more toward paranormal.

She has three former pound puppies that she dotes on and three daughters that she adores.

Rhiannon has lived in multiple states though she is currently residing in North Carolina. Wandering, witching, and reading with her puppies and husband are what she does when she isn't writing.

To learn about what is happening in Rhiannon's world and get loads of pupper cuteness, sign up for the by using the QR code below to visit my website.

Mercy of the Vampire King

Shame of the Vampire King

Pursuit of the Vampire King

Prey of the Vampire King

Reign of the Vampire King

Coming Soon

Love and Vampires Series

Olivia's Fall

Olivia's Prison

Olivia's Flight

Olivia's Family

Warriors of the Old Gods

A Dream of Blood

A Dream of Wolves

A Dream of Stone

A Dream of Ravens

A Dream of Bones

www.ingramcontent.com/pod-product-compliance
Lightning Source LLC
Chambersburg PA
CBHW030802190726
48285CB00003B/975